# THE SLEDGEHAMMER KILLER

A chilling crime thriller with a stunning final twist

EMMY ELLIS

*DI Bethany Smith Book 9*

**Originally published as *The Last Hurrah***

JOFFE BOOKS

Revised edition 2024
Joffe Books, London
www.joffebooks.com

First published in Great Britain in 2020
as *The Last Hurrah*

This paperback edition was first published
in Great Britain in 2024





Cover art by Dee Dee Books Covers

ISBN: 978-1-83526-170-5

# PROLOGUE

*I'm here, looking through the spyhole.*
*Watching. Checking. Starving.*

Remington stared at the rubble by his feet. He'd scattered it over the hole, which he'd created by smacking the concrete with a heavy mallet, the sort labourers used on building sites. The boss of him, Simon, had read an article in a magazine about it once, while he was in the cupboard, locked away. There wasn't much else to do in there, see. Simon had been lucky that Trevor, his stepdad, had allowed him to have the mag. Trevor wasn't usually nice.

She was under the ground, that woman, one of many who resembled Edwina. One who'd had to pay for what she'd done, for allowing Trevor into Simon's already chaotic and frightening life. It had got worse after he'd arrived on the scene.

Bastard.

All those who looked like her had to be killed. Simon said so. And what Simon wanted, Simon got.

Remington had to help the man out. Ease his tormented mind. While he didn't much like doing certain things, he realised it was necessary. In order for Remington to feel okay, Simon must feel okay.

It was a pickle really, all of it, but he had to continue, finish what he'd started.

He walked over to a different pile of rubble, another woman beneath it, although, given how much time had passed since he'd put her there, she had to be rotting by now. He'd bet she'd gone through the bloated stage already, where her body filled with gasses and liquid, then split in places from the pressure, that liquid seeping out into the ground.

It did smell around here.

People would probably attribute that to the nearby canal.

A figure approached from the darkness, giving Remington a bit of a start, and he almost let out a pathetic squeal. He'd chosen this time of the dark morning because everyone who hung out around here would be gone, but he'd misjudged it. Had the bloke been watching? Had he seen what Remington had done?

Smacking at the ground. Digging. Placing the body. Covering her up.

Christ. That wasn't good. Simon would be so angry if he found out.

Remington would have to keep that to himself. It wasn't good to get Simon angry, and there was so much anger there, Remington wasn't surprised it had burst out the way it had, resulting in . . . this.

"Want your usual, do you?" the figure asked. His voice was like Simon's, uncultured, showing which side of the tracks he'd been born on. He was a naughty person, this man, but necessary to mix with, if only for the brief moment it took to buy things. This fellow, he was from Simon's past, and they called him Runner.

Remington didn't like his accent. He tried hard not to speak that way. "Yes, please." It was best to say that, wasn't it, otherwise he'd have to explain what he was doing here, and that wasn't an option. Even though he didn't need anything at the minute, he'd buy it to make the bloke bugger off.

"What do you even need it for anyway?" Runner asked.

Remington shrugged. He needed a plausible answer. He searched his brain for why that particular drug was used. Yes, that would do, he'd give that story. "My girlfriend enjoys pretending we're in a 'certain situation'. You know, the sort Rohypnol's used for." He winked, then remembered Runner probably wouldn't see it. But maybe he sensed it. *Remington* sensed stuff like that. If he didn't, he'd never know people wandered around his house as if they had the right to be there.

"Some people are right kinky bastards." Runner snorted.

Remington wasn't kinky. He didn't go for any of that rude stuff. Simon had had enough of that to last him a lifetime, so Remington shied away from it, too. "Yes, there's a lot of us about." That was what you said, didn't you, to sound authentic?

"Bloody oddball." The drug dealer held his hand out, a tiny vial held between thumb and finger.

Remington ferreted in his pocket for some money, glad he'd brought his wallet with him. He must have had some foresight lurking in his mind earlier, letting him know he'd need dosh. He extracted some of the precious cash, withdrawn from Edwina's bank earlier in the day, and passed it over.

The vial was light in his palm, and he shoved it in his pocket with the wallet. Didn't hurt to have an extra supply. Who knew when he'd need it? Simon would insist Remington do another job, so it was handy.

"You're lucky I came out here," Runner said. "I'd been at the other location down the way a bit, you know, on the opposite side of the canal. By the other warehouse. Saw headlights here so came over, thinking someone needed my gear, and I was right. Usually am." He sniffed as if he'd enjoyed a bit too much of the white powder he'd offered Remington once.

"Glad you did." Remington smiled. "Saved me coming back tomorrow looking for you. Anyway, cheers, see you soon."

He walked to his car and got in, conscious of Runner staring. Once, Remington had seen him standing beneath a lamppost, one with a broken glass cover over the bulb, and Runner had seemed so scary, so *bad*. Menacing, nothing like the scrag he'd been when younger, according to Simon.

Remington drove off, worried and out of sorts. That happened sometimes, him off kilter, yet other days, he had *all* the courage and came off as cultured, that he had his shit together.

He wished that were true twenty-four-seven. Life would be so much easier then.

The journey was uneventful, and he thought about one of the plans he'd written down. *That* journey in the future wouldn't be uneventful. Quite the opposite.

At home, he entered via the back door and stepped into the kitchen. Victoria stood there, a questioning expression clouding her features, and he sighed. Why did she insist on turning up when he least wanted her there? She'd tried to fix Simon once, stop him from being so . . . so weird, but she'd failed. She probably wanted to fix Remington, too, with all her therapist mumbo-jumbo. Waffle, the lot of it.

"I'm not in the mood for a lecture," he said. "I just want a hot chocolate, a shower, and then bed."

"You need to stop this, going out at odd hours. You're as bad as Simon was. He used to do that an' all."

"I know, which is why I've taken over. Simon isn't as clever as me. He'd have got caught if he'd carried on. Anyway, stop bothering me. Go away. Just leave me alone. You're always trying to get inside my head. Make it all better. Well, I'm doing that fine by myself. I don't need your help."

Victoria seemed to float off to stand by the wall, her back pressed against it. Anyone would think she was attached to it. She always stood there when she wasn't on his arse for something or other, a sentry, some warden of his life, watching whenever he was in the kitchen.

Simon had got rid of her once, but she kept coming back.

Who'd have thought that could even happen?

# CHAPTER ONE

*Day One/Call One*

"DI Bethany Smith, how may I help you?"

"I've killed a woman. *I* did it, he didn't."

"Excuse me?"

"I'm going to be killing more. He said that's what I need to do."

"What's your name, please, sir?"

Dead line.

* * *

*Day Two/Call Two*

Bethany recognised the number. "Hello, sir."

"Hello, lady. Bethany."

*Oh God, he knows my name.* "Who are you? I need to know so I can help."

"You don't need to know who I am. What you *do* need to know is she's in the rubble, the woman I mentioned yesterday. Someone else is next."

"Where is her location?"

"I told you. In the rubble."

"But where is that?"

"You need to go out and find her." A pause. "*He* saw you on TV. And Mike Wilkins. I watched the news segment on YouTube."

Bethany's stomach rolled over. "Where is the woman, sir? The exact location?"

"You can't arrest him."

"Who is 'him'?"

"He's . . . Look, just leave him alone. He's scared you'll find him."

"I'm not interested in who that is at the moment, I need to find the woman."

"Don't bother. She's worthless."

* * *

*Day Three/Call Three*

"I like your house, lady."

"Pardon?"

"Your house. I like it. Red front door."

"Are you watching me?"

Laughter.

* * *

*Call Four*

"She wriggled."

"Who did?"

"The second woman."

"What do you mean by that?"

"She wriggled, like the first one, and the scalpel slipped."

* * *

*Day Four/Call Five*

DCI Kribbs stared at Bethany across her desk. "So he's phoned you at the same time each day so far?"

Bethany nodded. "Except yesterday, he rang me an hour after the first call."

Right on cue, her phone trilled, a different number on the screen, so she put it on speaker.

"DI Bethany Smith, how may I help you?"

"Why didn't you know it was me?"

*Shit, it's him.* "You've changed your number."

"Did I?"

"Please tell me where the women are."

"Rubble again. Number three is in the operating theatre."

Bethany's heart thundered. "She's in hospital? Because of you?"

"No, because of *her*."

Confused, Bethany frowned. "Her?"

"Yes, her. This is all her fault."

"Who is she?"

"Like the others. Not important. Your kettle is black and matches the toaster. Your silver microwave has crumbs and dust underneath it. You can see it when you bend low. Maybe clean it when you get home later."

"Have you been inside my *house*?"

"No, that would be breaking and entering. Number Three is crying. She needs the scalpel. Good day to you, lady."

He cut the connection.

Bethany let out a long breath. "What the . . . ?"

"He doesn't sound like he's the full ticket," Kribbs said. "So what's next?"

"We'll try again to find the owner of the phone number and get a location on this new number, but all the other calls were made from the estate I live on."

"So he's definitely at or near your house," Kribbs said.

"You heard him, sir. He knows I have crumbs and dust under my microwave, for God's sake."

"It's worrying. You said before that he mentioned seeing you and Mike on TV."

She nodded. "Does he have a fixation? Watched too many films where the detective becomes a target? How lovely, I'm living in a cliché."

Kribbs chuckled. "Seriously now, are you okay?"

She nodded. "A bit unnerved with him knowing the contents of my kitchen, who wouldn't be, but I'm more worried about the women. If he's to be believed, he's killed two and put them near rubble. We've been checking various places in Shadwell to determine where that is. So far, nothing."

"Hmm. An operating theatre. Do you think he's a doctor? That's twice he's mentioned a scalpel."

"How can he have access to a theatre if he isn't a doctor or surgeon? He said in one call the scalpel slipped, so we've checked with the hospitals and asked if there's been any accidents during surgery where that happened. Nothing." She shook her head, frustrated and lost.

How could she stop a man from murdering if she had no bodies to go on to get evidence from them — and no idea where and who the hell he was?

* * *

*Call Six*

"She looks beautiful now."

"Who does?"

"Number Three."

"Please tell me these women's names."

"I don't know them."

She had to see whether he was a real doctor or not. "So you're operating on them without reading their files?"

"Files? The only notes I have on them is that they all look like *her*. That's all I need to know. Have you checked missing persons? Surely someone's reported at least one of them as absent from their lives by now."

"Yes, we've checked."

"And?"

"Who are they?"

"You left a smear of butter on the worktop this morning after you made your toast. I watched it melt in a shaft of sunlight. Quite fascinating. Have a good day."

* * *

*Day Seven/Call Seven*

New number.

"Long time no speak, lady. Rubble. You still haven't found them."

"That's because I think you're a crank, messing with me. You're bored — and you're boring me." She'd said what Kribbs had advised, although she'd pointed out the caller could get angry if he thought she wasn't taking him seriously.

"Oh, I'm not messing with you. I have a new one right now. She's waiting in theatre. She needs to be beautiful."

"What do you mean by that?"

"Ribbons. She needs ribbons."

He ended the call.

Bethany left the incident room and walked to Kribbs' office. A tap on the door, then she entered. "Sir, he's changed call times. Just had another one."

Kribbs glanced at the clock. "So, the morning isn't working for him now? Perhaps he works shifts and this week it's the evening when he's free."

"He said he has another one — so that's a fourth woman. He mentioned her needing to be beautiful and have ribbons."

Kribbs stroked his chin. "For her hair?"

"We'll look into that. I'll ask Fran to stay on and check where ribbon is sold. Tomorrow, she can crack on with finding out how much has been purchased in various places."

"You're all doing the best you can." Kribbs sighed. "With no exact ping location, and different numbers being used, this is going to be a dead end unless he slips up or the bodies are discovered. You've tried Shadwell Hill, I take it?"

She nodded, thankful there was no rubble up there. She couldn't stand to find more bodies in the woods at the top. As no one had stumbled on the rubble or bodies so far, they must have been placed out of the way, a hidden location? "This is driving me round the bend, sir."

"I imagine it is."

She was tired, nervy, uncomfortable in her own home in case the man had been inside. A sweep had been done by a couple of officers from Forensics, and if she'd had someone prowling around inside, he'd left no fingerprints, hairs, nothing, so they'd deduced he'd just been looking through the window. Her kitchen was at the back, so he'd have climbed over the gate — she always kept it padlocked and bolted. No neighbours had seen anyone scaling it.

"I'll get back to the incident room then." She smiled and walked out.

Who was this man, and why had he chosen her to speak to?

* * *

*Day Eleven/Call Nine*

Bethany stopped writing mid-sentence and lowered the black marker to the small lip at the bottom of the whiteboard. The team had gone still, watching her to see if they needed to listen in on her call. Her phone had been set up to record her conversations. She looked at the screen. Nodded. Answered.

"How are you today, my good lady?"

Bethany sighed. "Please stop pissing about. You're wasting my time. I don't believe there are any bodies, no women who need to be made beautiful. No ribbons or rubble."

"Oh, there are ribbons, but I always fix them so they become lines."

His riddles, the way he was so vague, got on her nerves. "Lines?"

"I don't give them as many as *he* has. His lines are like wire mesh. They overlap."

"Listen to me. I'm no longer going to entertain you. I think you're a liar, a sick person who enjoys making up stories. You're a waste of time and space and—"

"Oh. You shouldn't have said that."

"Why not? It's what you are."

"No, it's what *he* is. I'm different. I'm worth something. I can be loved, you know."

"Who'd want to love a supposed murderer?"

"Someone will, you just wait and see."

"Please go and get some help. If this is how you're spending your days, you need someone to talk to. A therapist."

"Ha! I live with one of those. How amusing. I don't need help. *He* had it, but she didn't fix him like she promised. He shut her up for good in the end, you know, killed her, although she still stands there, butting her nose in."

"How can she do that if she's dead? See? You're wasting my time, like I said."

"I'm not. You'll have egg on your face one day. Maybe even bacon and sausages as well. The whole 'Whoops, I've made a massive mistake' meal. Enjoy the fry-up, woman. Eat what you cook and choke on it."

"You have a strange way of saying things."

"And you have a strange way of disregarding death. Still, we all have our foibles, don't we. Ta-ta for now."

* * *

The calls went on for months. Sometimes, seven days passed between his stories of women in theatre. One other time, a whole month. Bethany was on edge, waiting for him to jump out on her somewhere. She wondered if the fry-up term meant he'd show her he was telling the truth by grabbing *her* and taking her to theatre, giving her the lines and ribbons he was so fond of mentioning. Then she'd know he'd been telling the truth.

The problem was, while she had moments of believing he was just some nutter after attention, another part of her asked: *What if he isn't? What if he's really killed these women?* It was a difficult one. To believe or not to believe? For now, she'd agreed with her team that they'd treat it as real and just hope that at some point they'd find the bodies. Once that happened, they could get on with the task of identifying them — there were a few missing females listed, but whether any of them were his victims, it was difficult to tell without corpses.

They were stuck. There had been a breakthrough regarding the SIMs, though. Purchased in Shadwell, cash sales, various shops, all of them without internal CCTV, what a bloody surprise. Leona had studied the outside cameras and spotted men entering the shops, but although they were all the same height, some were fat, some slim, and every time, the faces were obscured by a scarf wrapped right up to below the eyes.

That was a significant piece of information. The man was disguising his body shape as well as his face — or were there two men, one larger than the other? Was there the man who called in, then the 'he' he'd spoken about?

Bethany didn't know, but what she *did* know was she was coming to the end of her tether. Living in fear of someone coming into her house at night while she was in bed, despite patrol cruising every couple of hours down her street, was taking a massive toll.

One night, while staring at the ceiling in the darkness, the sound of the radiators cooling down clonking in the quiet, she asked herself questions she'd been dreading throughout her career.

*Can I do this anymore?*

*Do I want to do this anymore?*

*How much longer can I put myself in danger?*

She knew the answers, just couldn't bring herself to say them out loud.

Something had to give, and she was buggered if it'd be her mental health put on the line. For now, she'd continue, but if the time came where she answered those questions out loud, that was it. She was gone. There was only so much even she could take.

# CHAPTER TWO

"This isn't a joke, Detective Inspector Smith. I fail to see why you find it so funny. The way you laughed like that tells me you're not taking me seriously. That isn't something I'd advise," the man said.

In the incident room, Bethany clutched the phone tightly, wondering who the hell this was on the other end of the line again. "I *don't* find this funny, far from it. I laughed because you've got a nerve keep calling me, wasting my time. You can be arrested for that, you know."

"Oh, I know. You'll have several nerves touched by the time I've finished with you. Especially if I decide to come and get your partner. I heard you rely on him. Mike, isn't it?" He laughed. "Yes, he's the key to getting you to listen to me, I do believe."

"Your threats are pointless," Bethany said, even though she was shitting bricks now Mike had been mentioned. "I have a job to do regardless of whether Mike is with me or not, so you suggesting you're going to 'get' him isn't going to upset me." The words burnt her tongue; they didn't feel right because they were lies. She loved Mike as a mate, and anything happening to him would destroy her. Shit, she'd almost lost her cool then, had wanted to call this bloke all the names under the sun for involving Mike.

"Oh, come now. Don't tell me you'd put your job over Mike in the importance scale. I won't believe you if you try to convince me of it."

"Look, what the hell do you want?" Bethany snapped.

She'd allowed her emotions to get in the way when she was supposed to be calm, keeping the man talking.

"You'll see, Detective, you'll see."

A click went off in Bethany's ear, and she cursed. She'd fucked up, well and truly.

"Shit. Shit!" She paced the room. "Don't say a word, all right? I know what I did. Next time—"

"You'd better hope there *is* a next time," Kribbs said.

They'd chosen to remain here long after the team had left for the day, expecting the call that had riled Bethany to the point of wanting to scream. It had been one of many where he'd given snippets of information that hinted something bad was going to happen but he hadn't said exactly what. Normally they'd ignore such calls — there were so many whack jobs around it was unreal — but this bloke knew too much about Bethany that it was clear he'd been watching her for a while.

*And if he's been watching me, he's been watching Mike. Jesus Christ.*

The worry of it all had shredded Bethany's nerves and had her seriously thinking of leaving her job. It was too much, the calls, the final straw in a bale she'd stacked, a defence mechanism, something she clung to, that stopped her thinking about her lonely life outside of work. It seemed the man ringing her had forced her to evaluate her world and decide what was more important — her mental well-being, Mike's safety, or solving crimes.

That was a joke. Solving crimes had contributed to her acting sane. Take that away, and what did she have? Regardless, she couldn't keep going like this. The caller had hinted she was in danger, and now he'd implied Mike was.

If it meant saving her partner, she'd quit, simple as.

"He'll ring again tonight, no doubt about it," she said.

On cue, the phone trilled once more. At Kribbs' nod, she pressed the screen for speaker.

"DI Bethany Smith, how can I help you?" she said in a bored tone, one they'd discussed she'd use so the man didn't pick up on any anxiety.

*Bloody failed there on the last call, didn't I.*

"Ah, I'm so glad you answered," the man said. "I thought for a moment you might have had to stomp off. You know, have a little tantrum because I'd dared to bring Mike into our conversation. Admit it, I hit a sore spot, didn't I?"

"Not at all." Bethany eyed the clock. "To be honest, I snapped at you because you're boring me. You clearly want something, so why not just come out with it so you can get the ball rolling on whatever it is you plan to do? You've been vague so far, and playing guessing games really isn't my forte."

"I detect testiness, dear woman."

"Like I said, it's boredom."

There was a five-second pause.

*He even has the bollocks to waste call time.*

"All right then, Detective. Let us begin on the latest thing. There is a woman's body. I'm not sure when you'll find her, I don't know anything about that yet, but find her you will. When you do, she might be already dead, she might not. Time and circumstances will tell. Good evening, lady."

The phone clicked again. Bethany swiped at her mobile, the thing remaining on the desk by luck not design.

"Fuck it." She shoved a hand through her hair. "So what do we do? Just wait until he calls again?"

"There's nothing else we *can* do. You and the team have already tried everything," Kribbs said. "I don't think he's going to telephone again tonight now he's stated his piece. He'll want you to stew, to worry over the woman — which you will, like you did with all the others he's told you about. So go home. Get some rest. Come back in the morning refreshed."

Bethany laughed. "Refreshed? You think I'll sleep now?"

"You have to learn to switch off," Kribbs advised. "Maybe I've been in this job too long. It doesn't affect me like it used to. When I leave here at the end of the day, I don't think about any of the cases."

Bethany wanted to say that with all due respect, Kribbs was nothing but a penpusher now, so of course he wouldn't take his work home with him. He didn't have to stare at dead bodies and search for their killers. He didn't have to look for murdered women who'd been dumped somewhere in Shadwell, coming to dead ends because the caller hadn't given her any locations, just stupid riddles that made no sense.

Six months of this. It wreaked havoc with her head.

Instead of replying, Bethany nodded. It was all she had the energy for. Arguing about them switching off or not wasn't going to do any good. And not sleeping wasn't going to do her any good either. She was between a rock and a hard place. Knowledge was meant to be power, but at this moment it was a lamp plug with a dead fuse. Fucking useless because there wasn't any light, only darkness so thick she'd never see her way through it.

She grabbed her coat. "Right. I'm off."

"See you at eight in the morning," Kribbs said. "If there's any more contact overnight, save the recordings so I can listen to them."

"Will do." Bethany grabbed her phone and left his office, telling herself to get the hell home and forget those insane calls.

That was a joke, though. They drove her around the damn bend. Being helpless wasn't something she handled very well. Nor was being played by some sick fuck who enjoyed dangling carrots then snatching them away just as she moved to take the first bite.

While she drove home, she thought about the man they'd dubbed the Creep, trying to piece together who he was. Cultured, well-educated by the sound of him, so he'd know a thing or two. Unlikely to make mistakes. That was already clear, the way he legged it from wherever he rang from so they couldn't get there in time once his burner mobiles had pinged the nearest tower. Mobiles. Again, a good move. SIMs could be bought for a tenner then thrown away. Mind you, Bethany wouldn't put it past him to mask his number before he made the next call, or have some kind of tracker blocking app installed so he didn't have the expense of buying new ones all the time.

*Shit.*

At a red light, she slammed the heel of her hand onto the steering wheel, setting off a short blast of the horn. The driver in the lane next glanced across, frowning, his expression that of a man asking *What the fuck's your problem?* Bethany resisted holding up her middle finger. No good would come of that either and, knowing her luck, she'd be caught on CCTV, which would result in a reprimand.

*Tell me why the hell I do this job again? Why I'm still here, looking for women I can't find? Answering the calls of a madman?*

In the past, she couldn't have left the force if she'd tried. She was married to it instead of her late husband, Vinny. Now, though, it was seriously close to her getting a divorce. She had a strong feeling she'd be filing the papers for it soon. You could only take so much, couldn't you, before you broke.

Who was the Creep, and why had he chosen her as the one he wanted to contact? Why not Mike, Fran, or Leona, the three others on her team?

*Because me and Mike have been in the papers. We're prominent, our names stick in the mind of the public because of the rate we solve cases.*

That bloody Peter Uxbridge from the *Shadwell Herald* needed to bog off. He'd sensationalised all the murders committed since Bethany had taken over the team, as if he wanted to rile her, needed to in order to get through the day.

Because of him, sometimes she got recognised in the street, what with having her picture on the news and online so often. It was insane, surreal, and she'd never get used to it. She wished it didn't happen, but Angela Hill, the editor, had run a flattering piece about Bethany and Mike, hailing them as heroes.

It had got them noticed.

*So that nutter who keeps ringing has chosen me as his plaything.*

Much as she liked the editor and understood her intent, she could brain her at the moment. Bethany's life had become unpleasant, the ghosts of the women tormenting her while she slept, seeping into her dreams and turning them into nightmares. They stood there holding rubble out to her, asking, "Find me . . ."

The traffic light turned amber then green. She drove off, eager to get home, going faster, pressing her foot to the floor and navigating the traffic like a nutter. She told herself to calm down, to ease off on the accelerator. A car came out of nowhere to her left. It slammed into the passenger side, shoving her vehicle across the road towards the verge. Bethany shouted a garbled sentence, her body going cold through fear.

Her car dived into a thick, high hedge then came to a halt. Bethany prayed no one had been hurt, an innocent person just walking home, or another driver. She sucked in a huge breath then let it out slowly, forcing herself to focus, to think of her training and what she should do next. She couldn't get out through her door, the hedge saw to that, but maybe the passenger side or the rear ones might work.

She reached over to try the passenger side. The door creaked open without her even touching the handle. Someone in a hooded top poked their head in, and although the interior light was on, Bethany couldn't see whether the person was male or female. And the face was obscured somehow.

*By a mask?*

The realisation of that kicked in, and she scrambled for her phone.

"Ah, no, my good lady. That isn't a sensible idea."

If Bethany thought she'd gone cold before, she was mistaken. A deep freeze plundered her body, and she stilled her hand, shocked to her core.

"I just crashed by to ask a question," he said. "You see this door here? How it's caved in? Imagine if I'd hit you harder. Imagine, dear, if Mike had been sitting there."

# CHAPTER THREE

*The Boy cringed, cowering on the floor in the corner. Being hit by Trevor wasn't nice, and it looked like a hit was coming, going by the severe expression on his face. He was angry, probably because of what the Boy had done earlier.*

*Or what he hadn't done.*

*"I swear to God, one day, I'm going to end up killing you." Trevor raised his fist.*

*It landed on the Boy's cheekbone, which had hardened over the years, the past couple of months especially, since Trevor had walked into his life and made it worse than it already was. Edwina had married him within two weeks of them meeting, saying he was her soulmate, her one and only.*

*She did things like that, on the spur of the moment. If she wanted to do something, she just did it, seemingly without fear of getting caught. She'd said once she didn't have a conscience, didn't 'give a toss about nothing', and would do whatever she saw fit, when she saw fit.*

*Including abusing her son.*

*"When your mother says to do something, you do it, right?" Spittle flew from Trevor's mouth. His eyes bulged, and his cheeks were a bit red, from anger, but maybe it was also from the booze he'd chucked down his neck.*

*The Boy didn't want to do what she'd asked, though. He was only seven and shouldn't have to work like she did. She called it work, or 'parties', but he didn't think it was. The customers gave her money afterwards. The Boy was supposed to stand in the corner of the bedroom and watch, but he hated it. Tonight, he hadn't cried like she'd asked him to, like he was supposed to.*

*Men came to the door and asked for the Crying Lad. Seemed he was famous around here, to bad men who did rude things to Edwina anyway. And it was weird, but although he hated it all, at least he was wanted. At least the men looked forward to seeing him cry.*

*"In the cupboard." Trevor pointed to it.*

*The Boy wondered whether he'd come into this room on purpose, knowing he'd have to go into the cupboard. It had a spyhole on the door, which Edwina and Trevor peeped through to make sure he was still alive. She said she couldn't be doing with the social services coming round if he ended up getting ill through starvation or he snuffed it. She'd be in trouble then, and besides, she wasn't suited to prison.*

*She deserved to be there, though.*

*He walked into the cupboard, with its sturdy door, a thick one, solid wood Edwina had boasted, so no kid like him could get out, even if he kicked at it. If you scratched it with your nails, you just got splinters for your trouble. There was a torch in there, more of a lantern really, hanging from a hook in the wall. The Boy had to switch it on if Edwina or Trevor told him to, so they could check on him properly. A dull silver, it emitted a bright-white glow, so bright it sometimes hurt his eyes.*

*Thank goodness he'd eaten all his dinner — fish fingers, chips, and a few baked beans; Edwina and Trevor, they weren't chefs — because that meant he wouldn't feel hungry until the morning. Tomorrow was Saturday. They could lock him in there for two days, and no one would notice.*

*Been there, done that.*

*"You can come out when we need you next. Tomorrow night." Trevor gave the Boy a shove, sending him flying into the cupboard wall.*

*The door closed.*

*The Boy cried.*

*He reached up to turn on the lantern, flicking the little ball on the end of the stick switch. The space illuminated, and he settled onto the brown velvet cushion on the floor to count the tiny squares on the wallpaper. There were so many, he'd never been able to add them all up. He usually fell asleep around the thousand mark. Each square had a dot in the middle, and although he hated that wallpaper, he loved it at the same time.*

*Strange, that.*

*If he looked hard enough, he managed to form pictures from the dots. A city skyline, a constellation, a knife, and even a scalpel, one of the tools he'd need if he were a doctor. Then came vials that held liquid drugs, needles and thread to stitch wounds together.*

*Once, he created a whole hospital.*

# CHAPTER FOUR

Remington. Now there was a good old-fashioned name. It fitted with his persona, the one he'd created for himself. The one that made him feel as though he belonged, was important. Not like Simon. Simon was a terrible little cretin.

Remington stared at Bethany, irked that there was no fear in the detective's eyes. Had the copper been trained so well that even the idea of Mike being crushed in a car accident failed to prod at her heart? Had her years on the force turned her to stone?

Simon knew all about covering up your emotions. Perhaps she was doing that right now. Hiding behind a steely facade to get through. When Simon was the Boy, he'd had to learn how to survive by concealing his feelings.

"Aren't you frightened?" Remington asked.

"Of what?" Bethany frowned, looking for all the world as if she were bored.

She was good at this. Good at putting on a mask.

"Of losing Mike, silly," he said. "He helps you so much at work, and he's your friend as well as your DS. It would be a shame if he were gone." Remington cocked his head — he'd practiced doing that in the mirror and thought he appeared quite sinister.

"Step away from the car," Bethany said.

*Ah, diversion tactics. Not facing her fears. If she loses Mike as well as her husband, she'll break. Shall I push her to that point or let her walk away?*

"I rather think I might." Remington glared. "But before I do, I just have to say that I'm not averse to killing men, you know. I've done it before. Who's to say Mike won't find himself subject to my scalpel?"

Bethany lunged across to the passenger seat. Remington stepped back, avoiding the copper's grasp. He laughed — he'd practiced doing that, too — and, pleased with how he'd sounded, he walked away from the vehicle. Bethany, if he guessed correctly, would be scrambling to get out now, or perhaps she'd be on her phone, calling in their encounter. Either way, it didn't matter to him. He got into his car, which he'd backed up after hitting Bethany's, and got on with the journey to his house.

Black BMW, false plates. Until he got home, of course. Then he'd put the original ones back on. Or another false set, depending on what he was doing, what Simon wanted.

He laughed again, happy with the night's efforts. He'd scared the detective, goaded her into acknowledging that no matter how hard she tried, she couldn't find the women.

Tomorrow he'd scout for another. He'd been on the lookout for a while now since he'd captured the bitch he'd just buried, but no one had caught his complete attention. There was always something wrong with them — their hair wasn't right, their eyes, their mouth. Still, he'd get what was needed eventually.

Remington pulled up onto his drive, to the right of the house he shared with his mother — *no, Simon's mother.* Edwina, that was her name, and Simon had called her that from as far back as he could remember. Because it annoyed her — and annoying her was what he'd apparently been born to do. She'd said as much a number of times. Plus, she didn't want to be reminded that she was a mum. Simon was a mistake, a slip-up, something that never should have happened.

He cut the engine and stared at the gate to the right of the house, set in a six-foot fence that he wished he could top with barbed wire, nails, and glass so no visitors could get in. That wasn't allowed, though, putting things like that on fences, and besides, it would draw unwanted attention.

So, the gate. It led to many things.

His home, different to the one Simon had grown up in, and it wasn't the same as this time last year since he'd revamped it more to his style, for his security and sense of well-being.

The memories. Although they hadn't appeared so often once he'd redecorated and changed the furniture.

And Edwina. She was still there — unfortunately — and it was about time she wasn't.

Simon had said Remington really needed to do something about her.

Remington got out of the car, clicked the lock, and looked across at the houses opposite. They were a funny lot around here, all former council tenants who'd bought their homes. He thought them funny because they were just like him, desperate to become someone else, to erase the stigma of living on an estate that used to be filled with rubbish and unsavoury people. No one here poked their noses into other people's business anymore — which was just as well, considering Remington was about to change his number plates.

With that job complete, and after he'd inspected the unfortunate dent in his front side panel, he entered the house via the back door and sucked in a breath of disgusting, rancid air. Simon thought the smell was lovely because of what it represented, and it reminded him of Trevor. Remington didn't. It meant he had more on his plate, dealing with the aftermath of what Simon had done. Remington wasn't prepared to take the blame for that one.

He locked up then walked through the kitchen and into the living room. Edwina sat in a chair similar to one that visitors used in hospitals — those placed beside every bed. Beige. Wooden armrests. It faced the TV displaying a family video, one of her favourites, because she liked to shout at Trevor when he appeared on the screen. The sound was loud, so he turned it down.

"Next door will complain about that if you're not careful, Edwina."

She didn't answer, but that was okay. He was used to her ignoring him, so one more time wouldn't matter. He preferred it. The grate of her voice brought on nightmares.

"You need a jolly good scrub," he said. "You smell horrendous."

He liked using Remington-type words. He sounded sophisticated. Horrendous was better than what Simon would say. He'd choose 'icky' or something equally as childish. Simon wasn't very clever. Probably all the times he'd been walloped on the head. Knocks like that sent you dumb.

"I shall wash you presently. Or perhaps tomorrow. It depends whether I get caught up with . . . things."

He made his way upstairs, needing to start at the top to check no one had come here while he'd been out. He didn't trust that someone else wasn't in the building. There was *always* someone else other than him or Edwina in this place. No matter how many times he caught them and made them leave, they kept coming back. That was why he wanted to doctor the fence. They couldn't climb over and get inside then.

He started with the bathroom. It was more of a wet room, something he'd been allowed to have because of Edwina. She'd struggled to get in and out of the bath, so having a shower room made things so much easier. The council had come and installed everything — *before* Remington had gone on to modify the rest of the place. He hadn't wanted anyone to see his interior design skills. They might well have reported him to the council, and his efforts would have to be removed. They didn't like you changing things without permission.

A red cord hung from one corner of the shower area, which connected to an alarm that buzzed when Edwina needed him. If she got into difficulty or whatever. He hadn't liked helping her, but what else could he do? She was Simon's mother and, as had been drummed into him countless times, he had a duty to look after her.

Remington didn't want to think about duty. *Simon* had a duty, not Remington.

Around the toilet, a set of what he thought of as monkey bars helped Edwina on and off the seat. The times Simon had cleaned her backside before he'd asked Remington to do it instead . . . Such a revolting job. It had become too much for Simon in the end.

The tiled floor was a pleasure to stand on, and the plain white shower curtain, when shut, gave the person under the water a sense of privacy. It was almost a replica of a hospital bathroom.

Funny, that.

As no one was in there, he moved on to the back bedroom. It used to be Simon's, what with it being the smallest, but when Remington had come along, he'd told Edwina she must have it now. Linoleum covered the floor — as it did in all the other rooms — the plain type that squeaked against certain kinds of shoe soles, the ones nurses liked putting on. There was the single bed, with the button on a cord down the side that electronically raised the head or foot, and the metal guard that prevented Edwina from falling out, and the white sheets, the waffle-weave blankets, the noisy, crackly pillows, and the curtains he could close around the bed, and the nightlight stuck to the wall, and the machine that gave her oxygen, and the . . . and the—

*Stop.*

Remington took a deep breath. Closed his eyes. Opened them to survey the room again. Yes, a proper little hospital he had here, every wall painted an insipid shade of mint green and even, wonder of wonders, a vending machine in the kitchen that dispensed hot drinks like they did in waiting areas. Above each door was a rectangular box that lit up at night, showing the word EXIT. He'd thought of everything, and having a hospital at home meant he never had to go back into a real one again. No. He'd never go back *there*. That was where Simon had lived. Edwina had moved to this house, out of Simon's childhood home, here for when he was let out.

In the next room, Remington checked everything was in order. It resembled Edwina's, except it was bigger, and he had one of those laminated over-the-bed tables on wheels that held a plastic jug for water and a stack of beige plastic cups. He also had a bedside locker, and inside there he kept a box of tissues and a baby's dummy for Simon.

That boy needed those things in an emergency.

Next, he went into the operating theatre, the spare bedroom. He declared that safe, too; there wasn't anywhere else that someone could be. He'd been through the kitchen and living room already, so where the hell were the visitors hiding?

"So pesky," he said, going downstairs. "They really do try my patience."

At the bottom of the steps, he inspected the front door. It still had the chain in place. He longed for automatic sliding doors, like the Emergency Department, but of course, that meant anyone could walk in, and that wasn't ideal. But he imagined the sliding doors there in place of the standard one he had, and that would have to be enough.

The imagination was a wonderful thing.

He'd created a reception desk of sorts in the hallway. All right, it was against the wall, and the top was only five inches deep, but the illusion was there. On top rested a signing-in book, with a pen on a string that was stuck fast with Blu Tack so no members of the public could steal it. He picked up the pen and smiled at the receptionist behind the desk. She was only a printout of some woman from a magazine, but she looked like one of the people Simon had known *there,* and Remington thought it fitting to paste her to the wall using PVA glue.

"Good evening, Della." He signed his name with a flourish then stated, in the narrow box provided, that he was there to visit Edwina.

"Are you not dropping in to see Simon tonight as well?" Della asked.

"Good God, no. Simon's . . . okay to be alone for the moment." The last thing Remington needed was to see *him*.

Della smiled. "Don't forget to sign out when you're done."

"I won't."

Remington walked into the living room. The fan of magazines he'd placed on the coffee table beside Edwina's chair hadn't been touched. So she'd let herself watch that rubbish on television for the whole time he'd been out, had she? And no one else had visited and read them — he'd seen that from the signing-in book.

"Really, Edwina. Don't you think reading *Good Housekeeping* would be better for you than subjecting yourself to this visual drivel?"

A man from a long time ago — a man Remington despised and who Simon had once been scared of — pranced around on the screen. He jived to the music at his and Edwina's wedding, showing off, expecting the guests to applaud him. The Boy stood in the background, looking all forlorn. He had his thumb in his mouth in place of a dummy. The man had confiscated it, saying that at eight years old, the Boy hadn't needed one.

Remington shuddered then switched his reaction away from what Simon would have done and into what Remington would do. He stuck his two fingers up at the man — '*Call me Trevor, not Daddy, because I ain't your fucking daddy!*' — then strode through to the kitchen.

And there, standing beside the vending machine, was a visitor. He *knew* someone was in here. He'd sensed it in the air.

"You didn't sign the book," Remington said. "Della won't be pleased about that. If you turn up for a visit, you sign in. Those are the rules."

"I *never* sign the book, you know that." Visitor Number One twirled her hair around a finger, exuding feminine wiles and giving him a come-hither grin, the same as she had the night he'd met her.

He hated that grin.

"No, you don't," he said. "And it isn't good. It means I have to make a note of you being here, so Simon doesn't get worried and come visiting, too."

"Are you close to finding another visitor?" she asked. "What are you on now? Twelve? Thirteen? There are so many, I've lost count. You could have quite a party if we all came back at once."

"None of your business whether I've found one." Remington moved to the vending machine. "I don't like it that you poke your nose into my life. You belonged in it for a while, because that was what Simon wanted, and then you had to go." He selected a hot chocolate, comforted by the sounds of the machine, whirs and mechanical shifts, the drizzle of liquid, the *pfft* as that very liquid created the froth that sat on the drink's surface.

"I didn't like it that you poked into my life either," she said, "but there you go."

Remington stared at her. She'd been his first. The skin on her face was a criss-cross of angry red slashes and squares where he'd lost his temper and tried carving her some new features so she didn't look like Edwina. It had gone wrong — so terribly wrong — and his knife had slipped, cutting a vein in her neck.

She'd . . . left him shortly after that.

"You must leave now I'm here," he said. "Simon will come back if you overstay your welcome, and I really don't want that."

"Simon wants you to make more visitors," she said.

"Yes, he does. But that's tough. Because Remington is here now, and Remington doesn't want to make them right at this moment."

He took the hot chocolate from beneath the spout. Lifted it to his lips. By the time he'd sipped then swallowed, Visitor Number One had gone.

# CHAPTER FIVE

*Trevor sold drugs for a living. He had a young lad working for him, Runner, so he'd called him. The Boy knew what Trevor did was wrong, same as Edwina's job, but he had no one to tell apart from a teacher. If he told, he'd get walloped. If he told, he'd get taken away to live with foster parents, who were much worse than Edwina and Trevor. They'd burn him with cigarettes and stab him with forks, starve him for longer, Edwina said so. He wouldn't be put in the cupboard but a damp cellar full of spiders and mice, and those horrible earwigs he hated so much.*

*So the Boy kept quiet and suffered in silence.*

*Runner stood in the living room, staring at his face in the mirror above the fireplace. He had spots with yellow tops, and his spiky hair was stiff with wet-look gel. The Boy watched him from his position on the floor between the sofa and chair. Kids like him, little fuckers, were only allowed on the floor. Little fuckers had to be seen and not heard, unless it was time to cry, then they could make a noise.*

*Trevor walked in, all swagger, and handed over a Tesco carrier bag. Runner opened it and pulled out a handful of smaller bags, transparent and filled with dried weeds from the indoor garden, which was in the spare room. The lights were always on in there, and the house smelt of the plants Trevor grew. The Boy wasn't allowed in while Trevor tended to them, but he was permitted to watch from the doorway, always with a warning of keeping his damn mouth shut about what Trevor was doing.*

*"Prime stuff, new strain," Trevor said. "Up the price by a fiver for a baggie."*

*"Right." The lad shoved the weeds away and scrunched the top of the carrier in his skinny fist. He picked at one of his spots.*

*"Fuck off then." Trevor shook his head.*

*Runner left, and the Boy wondered how old he was. He looked like a teenager, the way he was so 'gangly', something Trevor called him. The Gangly Twat.*

*"What are you fucking staring at?" Trevor asked.*

*The Boy jolted, afraid, his heart jumping. "Nothing."*

*"Nothing? Are you saying I'm nothing?" Trevor took a step closer. "You'd better not be, because you know what'll happen."*

*The Boy nodded. He'd have to go into the cupboard after he'd done his work.*

*"Let's do some employee training," Trevor said. "Come here."*

*The Boy scrabbled to his feet and walked out from between the furniture to stand in front of Trevor.*

*"Now, we're going to learn how to cry better." Trevor gripped the Boy's arm. "Ready?"*

*He pinched the back of the Boy's hand. It hurt, but he'd experienced worse. His eyes watered, stung a bit, but nothing like the sort of crying he was expected to do.*

*"That's a shit effort." Trevor dug his nails in.*

*The pain doubled, but only for a second or two, a sharp stab. Trevor twisted the skin, but it wasn't baggy enough for much movement, so he let go and grabbed at the Boy's side beneath his dirty T-shirt. Again, the hurt, but not enough.*

*"What the fuck can I do to make you cry proper tears, you little shit?" Trevor pinched even more, applying extra pressure. "That going to work? Am I going to see some of the old salty water dripping?"*

*The Boy bit the inside of his lip until he tasted blood.*

*"No? Well, then, let's try this." Trevor yanked the Boy's trousers down. "You can't tell me a pinch here won't get the floodgates open."*

*Tears came then, hot streaks down his cheeks, hanging from his chin, cold by the time they got there. Trevor was evil, a mean glint in his eye, his mouth wonky in a strange grin.*

*"That's better," he said, "but I want to hear some noise. Cry, you little bastard, cry."*

*He twisted.*

*The Boy choked out a sob, then another, and Trevor laughed.*

*"That's exactly what the customers want to hear," he said. "Remember that pain every time you're at work. I might even let you keep a pound if Edwina says you did good." He opened his finger and thumb, took his hand out, then shoved the Boy on the chest. "Now fuck off back to your place on the floor. You need to practise crying. There's an hour before the first man gets here."*

*Trevor walked out, and the Boy settled on the carpet. It throbbed where Trevor had pinched him. Proper tears fell, but not from any physical pain. They were the emotional kind, where he wanted to run away, be as far from Edwina and Trevor as he could get.*

*The problem was, he was stuck here. It was home, all he knew. A prison he hated, the walls enclosing him, hiding the horrors that went on inside them from the neighbours.*

*Did they know what Edwina and Trevor did to earn money? Did they care that the Boy was stuck here? He didn't know but hoped they didn't have a clue. Because if they did, it meant they were willing to let a child suffer. Willing to turn a blind eye.*

*And that would hurt more than any pinch, anywhere.*

## CHAPTER SIX

Bethany stood on the side of the road with PC Glen Underby, staring at her car being loaded onto a breakdown lorry. As well as Bethany, someone else had called the accident in. Glen and Tory Yates had arrived about five minutes ago, and Tory was now questioning an eyewitness down the road.

"This bloke is one hell of a twisted fucker," Glen said, hands in trouser pockets. "We come across some weirdos, but this man? Off his meds, I'd say."

"You're not wrong there." Bethany was still shaken up, much as she hated to admit it. "I didn't bother ringing Mike. Pointless worrying him about something he can do nothing about. And you know what he's like. He'd want to come down here."

"Hmm. Possibly what the Creep expected, you keeping it quiet. Means Mike's a sitting target at home." Glen shook his head.

"Fuck. I didn't think of that." Bethany kicked at the ground, sending a couple of loose pieces of tarmac flying. "Why didn't I ring him to warn him to be on his guard if someone knocked on his door?"

"Because, no matter how much you want to play the part of the big strong woman, you've had a bloody shock.

The mind doesn't process things the same after a fright, you know that." Glen sniffed, rocking on his heels.

Bethany wasn't going to argue the point. If she admitted to feeling shocked — unsteady, even — Glen might let it slip to someone else, then Bethany could be asked to take some time out. Now that she was involved in this case — personally involved — she was buggered if she wouldn't see it through to the end, despite wanting to run away and hide.

"I'm fine," she said. "Just pissed off I couldn't get out of the car quick enough to chase after him." She made a quick call to Mike. "Is your home alarm set?"

"Yeah," Mike said. "Why?"

"If someone comes round, don't answer the door. Explain later." With her mind at rest, she cut the call.

"Things couldn't have gone better for the Creep." Glen nodded at the car, now secured on the lorry. "D'you reckon he planned for the crash to happen that way, or that he just got lucky?"

"He definitely planned to ram the passenger side. Made his point nicely there." Bethany suppressed a shudder at the image of Mike sitting there, trapped and dead. "So we know he must have been close to the station when he rang me last. Had to have been to follow me, then cause this shit." She gestured to the car. Shook her head. "He's got some balls, I'll give him that."

"Knows what he's doing."

"And that's the frustrating part — he knows, we don't." Bethany wanted to punch something. "We just have to be drip-fed information as and when he sees fit. Knowing there's a woman out there with her name on his knife . . . shit, it chaps my fucking arse. This bloke's going to be the death of me, I can feel it."

"No, he's not. You're smarter than him."

"So smart I didn't even see the crash coming. So smart I can't find the previous bodies."

And *that* was the main bug. Bethany hadn't been concentrating while driving. She'd let her mind wander — and she could have died.

"Look, shit happens." Glen said. "In this job, we just have to do the best we can. We make mistakes like everyone else, what with being human and all that. So next time you'll be more vigilant. Lesson learnt." He paused. "Are you going to borrow a pool car while yours is being picked over?"

Bethany nodded. "May as well while I look for a new one. That bugger'll be a write-off. And it'll be in evidence for God knows how long."

"There is that. Still, there's bound to be trace left on it. Paint transfer, at least. And he leant inside, you said. Maybe dropped a few hairs while he was at it."

"The fucker had his hood up, and I think he probably had a hat on underneath. His type don't tend to make those kind of sloppy mistakes. And he wore a mask of some sort, from what I could gather, so no skin cells." Bethany swallowed. "He's got everything covered, I'd say."

"Got a bit of a job on our hands then."

"Yep, but we knew that right from the start."

"We did."

Glen was helping out on this case now along with her team. Fran and Leona had been working hard to find clues as to why Bethany had been targeted, all to no avail. Maybe it was just her being in the paper, like she'd first thought.

Tory walked over, slotting her notebook and pencil into the front pocket of her uniform. "One of the witnesses — Carl Duggins — reckons our man's been on this street before." She grimaced. "Carl walks his dog the same time every night and noticed the black BMW slowing as it passed him. He got the idea the driver wanted to check him out but didn't want Carl to see him. Not that he would have seen anything much — our man, like you said, was wearing a mask."

Bethany frowned. "And Mr Duggins didn't find that even remotely odd?"

Tory gave a weak smile. "Well, yes, but he didn't think it was something he should bother the police about."

That was the problem. The media screamed that calling the police was for emergencies only, when in reality, there were other numbers besides nine-nine-nine that could be used to report incidents. Yes, many people felt it best to mind their own business, but Bethany could think of too many times that a call reporting something a little off could have made a big difference.

"Right, well . . ." She puffed out a breath. "Nothing we can do about it now. Mr Duggins is aware he must call in if he sees the man again, I take it?"

"Yes." Tory's mouth downturned, as though she had more to say but didn't want to. "There's something else."

"Out with it then." Bethany gritted her teeth. She disliked dilly-dallying. Got something to say? Please just say it.

"When Duggins saw him a while back, the BMW driver pulled over, near the spot you crashed, then got out and walked round to the passenger side of his own car. He opened the door, stuck his head in, and appeared to be talking to someone. Except no one else was in there."

*What the hell?* "Like he was acting it all out beforehand."

"Seems that way."

"And again, Mr Duggins didn't think *that* was weird?" Glen asked.

"He did, but he said the man frightened him and he didn't want to say anything to anyone."

"Frightened, as in, how?" Bethany peered over Tory's head to where Mr Duggins had been. He must have gone home.

"Not an actual fright — a verbal threat or whatever — just a feeling inside him." Tory took her hat off to scratch her head. "He said he knew he shouldn't tell anyone, as though the BMW driver had actually said as much, even though he hadn't."

"I can understand his reluctance," Bethany said, "but shit, I wish he'd reported him."

"Would have been the luck of the draw as to whether one of our patrols spotted him if Duggins *had* reported him, though." Glen let out a ragged breath. "We're thin on the ground, so sending a car out to watch for him here wouldn't exactly have been on our priority list anyway. We wouldn't have known it was the Creep at the time either."

Bethany couldn't dispute that. She was clutching at straws, trying to envisage things being different. There was no point in it. They had to deal with what was on the table, not what *could* have been there. This feast of bullshit had filled their stomachs but left them hungry for pudding, which was finding the women.

"Fuck this," she said. "I need to go home. I'll fill out a statement in the morning — against protocol, I know, but sod it. I'm tired. It can wait. Will one of you give me a lift?"

"I'll do it," Glen said.

"Tory, can you deal with the scene here — get a couple of uniforms to help out with mapping the skid patches on the road and whatever." Bethany managed a smile.

"Okay." Tory looked at Bethany. "I hope you get some sleep tonight." She walked away, talking into her radio.

Bethany followed Glen to the patrol car.

They made the journey to her house in silence, Bethany staring into the wing mirror to make sure they weren't being followed. The closer to her home they got, the more worried she became. What if they turned the corner and blue lights flashed outside? What if that crazy fucker had gone there and the security alarm hadn't deterred him?

Nothing was happening outside her place, though. Bethany sighed out her relief. Everything appeared as it should. But that didn't mean nothing was going on *inside*.

"Want me to come in with you?" Glen asked.

"Might be a good idea."

Glen parked, and she got out, leading the way. At the front door, she steeled herself to find the worst. She walked inside then disengaged the alarm. Listened for any sounds that someone else was there.

No one.

Glen cleared the house, then left, and Bethany phoned Mike.

"Everything all right?" She bit her bottom lip.

"Why wouldn't it be?" he asked.

Relief poured into her. "I had an accident on the way home."

"What?"

"I'm fine, that isn't the issue. The issue is that I was followed by the Creep when I left the station after he rang in twice, and the crash was deliberate."

"Fucking hell . . . He needs stopping."

"Yep, he insinuated you're in danger."

"Me?"

"Hmm. Maybe we ought to bunk up together until we catch him."

"That's been difficult so far, catching him."

"Yes, but we have to keep trying. Glen's going to run the Creep's car make through the database, see what comes up. By tomorrow, uniforms will be out knocking on the doors of people who own black BMWs. The usual drill. Other than that, we just have to wait until he calls me again."

"What if he doesn't?"

"He will. He's too far into this scheme of his to stop now." She explained what had happened after the crash, plus what was said in the recent phone calls.

"So him speaking to you like that — shit, he's one brave bastard. Who pokes their head into the bloody car?"

"He's . . . so sodding weird. His voice — he's posh, yet he was wearing a hoody and what I thought were jeans." Bethany laughed wryly. "Listen to me, a copper who only *thinks* the man was wearing jeans. My observation skills are clearly fucked."

"You were probably scared." Mike paused. "Weren't you."

"Yes, I was scared. And I'm giving you fair warning. This is getting too much. I don't know if I can take it for an extended period of time. It's already been months he's toyed with us."

"We'll come out the other side of it like we always do. Stick with it."

That was easy to say, but Mike wasn't hanging by a thread, one that was likely to snap at any time. She dangled over an abyss, normality at the top of an overhang that represented a decent life, while below, the Creep waited in the darkness, ready to gobble her up.

# CHAPTER SEVEN

*The Boy stared ahead, fixing his attention on the wall above the bed. It was better that way, so he didn't see what happened. Edwina was working with one of her clients, who'd requested he stand and watch.*

*The Crying Lad.*

*They paid extra for that, and Edwina could buy a new dress or some fancy shoes with it. Or Trevor bought red wine for himself, vodka for Edwina for after the night had ended, and they'd drink themselves silly.*

*They laughed a lot then. Great bellows that kept the Boy awake.*

*Hopefully, he'd be in his bed tonight, not the cupboard, although sometimes, when Edwina and Trevor argued, the Boy took himself to the cupboard anyway, where it was safer, quieter. Okay, they could open the door, same as they could with his bedroom one, grab him by the hair, yank him out, and kick the shit out of him, but . . .*

*He let the tears fall. This client liked it if he cried without sound, just the tears. As well as the extra money for Edwina, he handed the Boy a tip, a few quid that remained in his hand for all of a few seconds, then Edwina snatched it away, making out she'd put it in his bank so he could save for the remote-control car he'd been banging on about.*

*He hadn't banged on about anything. Edwina was good at lying. And he didn't have a bank account. That money went into her pot on the mantelpiece, the metal one with roses all over it. That was where the 'spare' cash went, used for special treats.*

*Not that the Boy ever got any. But Trevor had mentioned him maybe getting to keep a pound, so that had kept him going through the past twenty minutes.*

*Edwina and the man had finished now, and a five-pound note was stuffed into the Boy's sweaty fist.*

*"Get yourself some sweets with that, kid." The customer walked out, doing up his trousers, leaving behind a creepy little laugh and the scent of his body odour.*

*The door closed.*

*Edwina held her hand out, and the Boy gave her the money. He didn't tell her about the pound. But he'd imagine what he could buy with it in the meantime. Sweets, lots of sugary sweets.*

*"Come and brush my hair for the next man." Edwina put the fiver on her chest of drawers. "Can't be looking all bedraggled when he first comes in, can I."*

*The Boy collected the brush and approached the bed, his cheeks stiff from dried tears. He wanted to hit her with the brush, slap it on her scalp, the hard part of it, not the bristles. It was good to dream sometimes, to imagine himself hurting her. Getting her back for everything he had to go through. Most boys at school, they said they loved their mum, but the Boy hated his. Once, he'd dreamt about heating up the sandwich toaster and pressing the boiling plates to her cheeks. Listening to the skin sizzling. Listening to her screaming. And she'd raise her hands to grab his wrists, try to move him away from her, thus moving the toaster. Her face would be a mess, cooked flesh, skin yellow and bubbling from the scorch.*

*Little lads shouldn't think things like that, his teacher had said so when she'd read one of his stories once about a clever elf who stabbed his wicked witch mother. There was blood and gore, her exposed heart thumping away on her wrecked chest, and even then, while dying, she cast a nasty spell on the elf. Always having the last word.*

*"That's it, nice long strokes. One hundred of them," Edwina reminded him.*

*He didn't need reminding. He knew what he had to do.*

*He vanished inside himself and got on with the task, thinking of the elf and how many different ways he could get rid of the witch.*

*He smiled.*

# CHAPTER EIGHT

Remington was glad he'd bought the sucky thing in preparation. On the website it had claimed to pull out dents without any trouble, as easy as one, two, three. The problem had been that he'd had one big dent decorated with many smaller ones. The sucky had dealt with it so well, though, like the magic device the advertising had proclaimed it to be. It had sorted the big dent in two or three pulls, then each smaller crinkle. Okay, it was still obvious, if you looked closely, that he'd had a prang, but for the most part, it was a passable fix.

He stood back in the darkness of his driveway in front of the hedge to inspect the bumper again. A few more goes, and he reckoned it would be almost completely smooth. What he hadn't figured in his plans was that he'd have to respray. The original red was showing through in places. He'd have a word with Simon about that. Simon should have warned him he'd used subpar paint that came off easily. Probably just bought the cheap stuff instead of shelling out that bit extra for a quality product.

"But not to worry," he whispered. "I'll have that fixed in a jiffy, no thanks to Simon."

Glad the sucky thing hadn't been overly loud — only the larger dent popping back out had created a bit of a bang

— he walked from behind the bush and checked the street to ensure the noise hadn't woken anyone up. Everything seemed as it should be, no lights on anywhere, no one peering out to see what the kerfuffle was, everyone tucked in their beds, good citizens living near a killer, oblivious. He collected the can of black spray from the boot then went to work. He'd have to buy some more if he decided to run Bethany off the road again. This can was almost gone.

As he covered the red, and the wonderful black took its place, he thought about Visitor Number One. She had a naughty habit of coming to the house more than the others, and he wondered, if she'd had such a terrible time with him like she'd said, why she kept returning. The others only drifted by every so often, probably too traumatised to come back each day.

*Maybe she loves me.*

The idea of that . . .

Remington could be loved, couldn't he? It was only Simon who couldn't. Simon was unlovable — he didn't have one redeeming quality, according to Edwina. Remington wondered whether the visitors and Simon's need for him to find them were for just that — love. Simon's therapist, Victoria, had suggested as much, but Remington didn't think that was the case. Remington was sensible enough to know that love didn't grow on trees, and it certainly didn't manifest as soon as you brought an alive visitor home. You had to *fall* in love, so the films and books said, and to do that you needed time.

Unfortunately, with every visitor so far, he'd tried to get them to love him, to give them a beautiful face instead of a slashed-up one, and they'd died on him. That was why he'd told Bethany about the women — and that they might be found dead. Remington didn't think, no matter how hard he tried, that his efforts at creating beauty would ever work out.

Edwina had said a slashed face was beautiful.

He finished off with the spray. "Simon makes me kill them. It's part of the deal." He admired what he'd done and found it perfect. "But I'm fully in charge now, so when I find the next woman, she'll remain alive."

He placed the can back in his boot then locked the car. "Perhaps I should tell Bethany that."

He entered the garden, then the house. He locked the door in an attempt to keep the visitors out, but they always managed to get in regardless, as if they could float through the doors or something, which was odd and not doable, yet they did it. The vending machine called to him, offering a cup of tea this time. He set the machine to go into action while he washed his hands. A bit of paint had got on his finger.

"I've changed my mind. I don't think I'll tell Bethany. At least not yet," he told Victoria, who stood to his left.

Her face was a picture pasted to the wall like Della the receptionist's, but her whole body was on show, one he'd drawn himself with a thick marker. Arms, legs, a torso, and that place in the middle, the dirty place. It had hairs on it. Curly ones.

"Don't you think that's a good idea, Victoria?"

"Yes. Very good. Perhaps tell her only if the beauty process goes wrong. If it doesn't, then you can enjoy having your visitor live with you and love you. What do you think about that?"

"Marvellous." Remington dried his hands on a tea towel.

"No matter what Edwina told Simon, he *is* loveable. You need to understand that, too. If you could just believe it . . ."

Remington stared at her.

She snapped her mouth shut, but not for long enough. "What I've been meaning to ask, though, is why you contacted the detective in the first place. Simon said what you're doing for him must remain a secret. He said you couldn't tell anyone because it brought the risk of getting caught."

Victoria was a nosy old bean, always in his business. It was a good job he knew she meant well, otherwise he'd get quite cross with her, like Simon had.

"Oh, you know." Remington walked over to pick up his tea. "The night I decided to contact Bethany, Edwina had the TV on, and it was a news piece about Bethany and Mike. Simon got a little afraid of being caught — the news was about Visitor Number One, months ago, going missing. That was when he decided to move out and pass the job to me. So I made contact, to see if Bethany was the type to find Simon, you know, so I could put his mind at rest. She doesn't sound as though she's interested in him. She isn't even interested in me." Remington waved a hand in the air. "The woman acts positively bored, and even though I ran her off the road, she was as cool as a cucumber." He shivered. Simon had told him Trevor used to say that.

*I'm cool as a cucumber, boy.*

Victoria frowned. "I see. I still don't fully understand, though. Wouldn't contacting Bethany put *you* at risk?"

"No," Remington barked. "It would put *Simon* at risk, and to be honest, they can take him away for all I care. He'd be out of my life then, and I could stay here and love my next visitor. It's Simon who gets me into all this trouble. I should never have got hold of the police, I realise that now. I was trying to *help* him."

Victoria had pressed his panic button. These were things Remington didn't want to discuss. It made everything confusing, thinking about Simon. Remington had telephoned Bethany. He thought he had things straight in his head, but Victoria or Della pointed stuff out and put those dratted spanners in the works. He'd most definitely been the one to run Bethany off the road, but maybe he'd imagined it because Simon had explained the scenario to him so many times. But Remington had fucked up. Simon wouldn't want the detective to speak to Remington — or vice versa. He hadn't said that was allowed.

Yet another thing to keep from him.

Remington's job was to get rid of all the women who looked like Edwina. He could do this so long as people didn't poke their noses in.

"Are you sure you can control Simon?" Victoria asked.

Her question sent Remington into anxiety mode. No, he wasn't sure, but he'd be damned if he'd admit that to her. She'd do something with his tablets, writing all about him on his notes, saying he'd had an 'episode' like Simon always had. And then where would he be?

"I don't want to speak to you anymore tonight." He walked to the doorway between the kitchen and the living room — the living room that was filled with the stench he so detested.

"You know, Edwina, I thought Simon would come back to deal with you, but at the same time I had a feeling I'd have to do it. He's so incredibly flaky. Unreliable. I'd ask him to fix his mess, but really, I don't want him here ever again." He sipped some tea. "I've finished my jobs for the night, so I'll prepare the wet room for you."

Upstairs, he took some bottles of disinfectant out of the cupboard beside the sink and sat them in a row along the shower wall. In a cupboard on the landing were stacks of towels, old ones left over from when the house hadn't been a hospital, just a normal home. He'd use those to dry Edwina — having the pristine white ones touching her wasn't something he thought he could bear. They'd get ruined. He'd bought them and renovated the place using Edwina's savings. She had no clue he'd stolen her bank card from her purse. Too busy staring at the TV, the silly cow.

He returned downstairs to stand in front of her. She was staring at the TV again. What she found so fascinating he couldn't fathom, but her mouth always hung open as though she was in awe of the information coming her way. She let her tongue hang out, too. And her eyes bulged — she really couldn't get enough of those flickering images.

"Deary me." He wished he'd thought to stick a peg on his nose so he didn't have to smell her. Her aroma had got steadily worse the past few days. "Simon really has a lot to answer for."

He hauled Edwina standing, the weight of her sending him off balance for a moment, the press of her body against his foul and frightening. He didn't like her this close, in his space. She was limp, and as he hefted her over his shoulder, he spotted that she'd soiled the chair.

"That's such a dirty thing to do," Edwina said. "Such a dirty, filthy fucking thing. You shit on the chair and think it's me, don't you? You're going to tell me this is my fault, when it isn't. It's Simon's. I was left there for ages, because neither of you bothered with me. You know I can't get upstairs on my own to use the toilet. Horrible, you two are. Wicked."

Remington blinked, alarmed at what Edwina had said. She sounded the same as she had when Simon had been little, all spite, her words striking at his heart.

"This is Remington you're speaking to, Edwina, and those sorts of mean words don't affect me. If you want to hurt, you need to say this to Simon. I'm just here doing what he wants. I don't care for your opinion." He carried her upstairs, wavering from her weight, almost toppling backwards. "However, Simon will never be here for you to say it to him, so please refrain from speaking such vile things. You're wasting your breath."

There, that felt better, to say that to her. He laughed at her saving her breath. Maybe she would if she had any.

Edwina stayed silent — he'd been expecting her to carry on regardless, so perhaps he'd frightened her into keeping her thoughts to herself. At the top of the stairs, he almost dropped her, his stomach going south at the thought. Although these stairs were on the other side of the house to the neighbour's adjoining wall, her thumping onto every step on the way down would be pretty loud in the middle of the night.

In the wet room, he placed her on the floor then positioned her so she was on her back. Distaste for what he was about to do roiled in his belly, but he had to undress her in order to get her clean. Simon had insisted she was washed before Remington delivered her elsewhere. The smell of her really wasn't acceptable any longer, neither was her presence. Simon had wanted to kill her ages ago, but his stint in the hospital had meant he hadn't been able to. He'd been there years.

As he stripped her, he mentally told Simon off for putting this all on him. Not only did he have to clean Simon's mother, but also the chair and the area surrounding it. Victoria could have done that instead of hanging around by the wall, but if he asked her why she hadn't, she'd claim to have been busy, and Della had said she wasn't employed as a nurse or porter, just a receptionist.

Everything always fell to him these days.

Job done, he put the clothes in a stinking pile. They had various stains on them — red, brown, some black specks. He pressed the button to start the shower. He'd get soaked while he washed Edwina, but there was nothing he could do about that if he wanted to do it properly.

First, he scoured her with the toilet brush to get off some caked-on substance that didn't bear thinking about. He doused her liberally with liquid soap, and the sight of the lather had him feeling so much better. Lather meant you were clean. Lather represented purity.

Once he'd done that and all the bubbles had floated down the drain, he poured disinfectant on every part of her. Why didn't she wince when it splashed over her face? Surely those cuts had to sting now that he'd scrubbed the scabs off.

She didn't make any sound at all, just let him get on with it, which was strange. Normally, according to Simon, Edwina had far too much to say for herself. Remington wondered whether Simon had lied about that, because since Remington had been in charge, the woman hadn't said that much. The odd flurry of spite here and there, nothing to write home about.

"You were pale a couple of days ago and very bloated, as though you were a balloon filled with water," he said. "Now it seems you've lost a lot of weight. Or that water has drained out of you, but how is that possible?"

He opened another bottle of disinfectant and sprinkled it on her cheeks. Still no wince or any reaction at all. He poured some into her mouth. *Still* no reaction.

"Well, I do believe all the fight has gone out of you, Edwina."

While he continued cleaning her, he thought about that missing water she'd had in her body. Where had it gone? Perhaps that was what the mess was on her chair and the floor. Had the bloaty liquid literally dripped out of the pores in her skin?

"Quite vile if that's the case." He checked her over to make sure he hadn't missed any skin. It all had to be properly clean before he could move on. "Righty ho, we're finished." He switched the shower off. "I'll just leave you here for a while, to dry naturally for a bit. I'll be back to wrap you in the towels. *Then* I'll take you out for a ride in the car. You'd like that, wouldn't you?"

"Fuck off, Simon."

"Um, no. This isn't Simon. You're getting confused in your old age."

He left the room so she couldn't argue with him. He didn't like her spouting rubbish at him. It brought back Simon's memories, and that was never good.

Downstairs, he allowed the vending machine to persuade him into having another drink. Coffee, it insisted. Something to keep him awake, give him the energy to do the task at hand, and quickly, as there were only so many nighttime hours.

"All right, a coffee. You're so good to me."

While the machine did its thing, he walked over to Victoria, who stood against her wall. "When Simon was here last, he said . . . Simon has assured me that him removing Edwina's fingertips, and her teeth, will go some way to stalling anyone who should want to find out who she is. Do you have any other advice? I'm doing what he should have done, and I really don't want to get the blame for taking her out of the house and putting her where Simon wants her to go. But she smelled so *ghastly* . . ." He pinched his nose between finger and thumb. "I had to do something about that, you understand."

"Cement," Victoria said. "Blocks of it. Attached to her feet."

Remington frowned. "Are you suggesting what I think you're suggesting?"

She nodded. "It's the only way to keep you safe from doing Simon's . . . activities. If she doesn't float, she won't be found. You can't do the rubble anymore. That drug dealer might start getting suspicious if you turn up there again after only just seeing him."

Remington nodded, too. "Oh dear. Honestly, this is becoming a bit of a bind, but I must say I'm exceptionally glad I listened to Simon and kept some of those chunks of cement from when this house was renovated." He wandered over to take his coffee out of the machine. "So it's the canal itself, after all — thanks for the suggestion. Simon implied it would be anyway. Did you know all the visitors also went in that area and have yet to be discovered?"

"Hmm. The spot he picked for them was perfect." Victoria smiled an encouraging smile. "Only fitting the original one goes there as well."

Remington sipped some coffee, the image of Edwina's wrecked face coming to mind. The slashes were gross and open, gaping. "He really did a shocking job at trying to make her look beautiful, you know."

"Yes, I know."

"What I don't understand is, how come Simon didn't die when Edwina made *him* beautiful?"

"Oh, that's easy. Edwina didn't nick the main artery in Simon's neck. You and him, though . . . You cut them there. Anger — it gets the better of people sometimes. I'm thinking, when you pick up your next visitor, that you'll be much more careful."

"Yes, I will."

Remington turned his back on Victoria and finished his drink. The hours had sped by already, and he just about had enough darkness left to drop Edwina off to where Simon wanted her to be.

Honestly, if he saw Simon again, he'd have stern words with him. This disposal malarkey really wasn't cricket.

# CHAPTER NINE

*Trevor let him have the pound the next day. The Boy clutched it in his tight fist, running towards the shop at the end of the long street where he lived, the houses whizzing by, slim Victorian efforts, all painted different colours — white, cream, blue, pink, grey. Someone hung out of an open sash window, smoking, flicking ash to the pavement below. Mrs Saunders, her name was, and she was older than Edwina and wrinkled, sometimes staring at him as if she felt sorry for him.*

*"Going to the shop?" she shouted, her black hair wavering in the breeze.*

*He slowed to a stop and looked across the road at her. "I'm going to buy some sweets."*

*"They'll rot your teeth, don't you know that?"*

*He didn't care if they did and his teeth fell out. He'd earnt them.*

*"Get me a pint of milk and a loaf of bread, will you?" She sucked on her fag then blew the smoke out. "Wait there while I get my purse."*

*She disappeared, the net curtain swinging, and he walked over to her front door. It was the nice kind, that white plastic stuff, nothing like the weathered wooden one his house had. It had a shiny silver handle and letterbox, plus a knocker with a lion's head on it, the ring passing through its mouth.*

*She flung the door wide and flicked her fag out into the gutter. "Here, and you can have fifty p for going." She handed him a fiver. "I want the receipt an' all."*

*Fifty p! He took the money, nodded, and shot along the path, working out how much more he could buy now he had extra. His legs had wings, his heart full of happiness, and for this moment, so fleeting amidst the never-ending days of summer at home without school to pass the time, he was free and content, excited even.*

*In the shop, he grabbed a basket, got her milk and bread, then stood in front of the sweet stand. Freddo bars were cheap, so he'd have a couple of those, and there were the twenty pence bags of sweets, like cola bottles, strawberry lips, and white chocolate buttons with little multi-coloured balls on top. He ended up getting loads and paid the man behind the counter, the surly Mr Badesh who always gave him filthy looks, like he suspected him of stealing stuff. His son was nice, though, he was in the Boy's class, but Mr Badesh's brother, he sometimes came to the house and vanished into the bedroom for a party with Edwina.*

*He never wanted the Crying Lad to come in.*

*Money handed over, the goods in a thin, pink-and-white-striped bag, the Boy took the change and the receipt and flew back up the road. He knocked on Mrs Saunders' door, lifting the bread and milk out and holding them high. She opened up and stared down at him, a frown wrinkling her forehead.*

*"Do you want some lemonade?" she asked. "You look a bit hot and bothered."*

*He glanced down the road, towards home, working out whether it would be all right. Edwina and Trevor were asleep — they'd worked late the night before, until well after midnight. Runner had come round for another bag of dried weeds about eleven.*

*"Okay," he said.*

*She stepped back to allow him in, and he followed her to a bright kitchen that was clean and nothing like the one at home. No crumbs on the worktop. No dust on the windowsill, which instead sported a potted plant with yellow flowers.*

*"They're pansies," she said. "Pretty, aren't they?" She took some lemonade from the fridge and poured a glass. "There you go."*

*"Thank you."*

*He sipped, standing by the door, looking around at all the things she had that they didn't. A shiny white fridge-freezer that was much taller than him. A black cooker with a silver hob, no bacon fat splashes or oil from fried eggs. Nice tea towels without stains, pinned to the wall like pictures. They had plants on them and names beneath. Thyme, basil, garlic.*

*He wished he lived here.*

*"Sit down if you like," Mrs Saunders said.*

*He jumped. "I need to go home." He swallowed the lemonade fast, the bubbles fizzing on his tongue and throat. It was cold on the way down, hitting his empty belly in what he imagined was a splosh.*

*"Doubt your mother will be bothered where you are." She sighed. "If I'd been lucky enough to have a child, I wouldn't treat him like this."*

*He didn't know what she was on about and shrugged. Placed the glass in the washing-up bowl. "She'll be hacked off if I stay out too long."*

*"Does she hurt you? Smack you if you're naughty?"*

*His stomach rolled over, and he shook his head.*

*"Hmm." She flattened her lips together. "Okay."*

*He ran into the hallway, fumbling with the lock on the front door, strangely uneasy and wanting to get out, get back home. Odd, when home was so frightening, yet here he was, desperate to be there, safe from prying questions and the look in Mrs Saunders' eye.*

*At last, he was outside.*

*"You come to me if you need anything," she called as he legged it up the road.*

*"Yeah!" he shouted back, his carrier bag bouncing against his thigh with each step.*

*Much as he'd like to tell her everything, he couldn't risk being placed with those wicked foster people. Better the devil you know, Trevor once told him, his face so close to his that their noses almost touched.*

*Yeah, better the devil you know.*

# CHAPTER TEN

Remington wasn't a happy bunny. The canal was letting off quite a stink, more so than Edwina, and that was saying something. Had another person disposed of rubbish and it was rotting, the stench pushing up out of the water and spoiling the air? Or was it the women beneath the rubble?

"Absolutely revolting."

He held his nose and scoped the area for signs he wasn't alone. He didn't want to get caught doing Simon's dirty work. The last thing he needed was Runner turning up again.

"This is the last time, Simon, do you understand?"

Somewhere in the recesses of Remington's mind, Simon's breathing pulsed, filling him with a sense of urgency. Things Simon had said or did always popped out every so often, as if Remington's brain conjured them and played them on repeat, slipping through some kind of unseen veil.

"Look, if I feel this way, I'm liable to make mistakes, and my deed will be discovered. I'm trying to help you out here, Simon. The least you can do is shut up and let me get on with it."

No one except him was at this stretch of the canal, he was sure of it. Safe in the knowledge that he'd remain undetected, he walked the three steps to his car and opened the boot. The interior light snapped on, illuminating his cargo. There was Edwina, wrapped up like a sausage in a bun, except the bun was made from the old towels, not bread. The light gave her cheeks a yellow tinge, as though she suffered from liver problems, and some of the staples in her face glinted. He'd used a stapler to hold the slashes together before he'd wrapped her up. Anything to diminish the sight of those ugly slices. Her lower half was folded so she fitted in the small space, but the top half . . .

"I should have covered your face, Edwina. At least your hair. Now strands of it may well be left behind. Another job to do before the morning comes then." He huffed out a breath, angry that getting to his bed wasn't going to happen any time soon. "I'll have to clean out the car when I get home."

At the rear of the boot, clumps of concrete formed a crude wall, the largest pieces he'd been able to find from the pile of rubble in the back garden. Wrapped around each piece were strands of pre-cut slender rope, forming a cross. The hunks of cement reminded him of wrapped presents, the rope used in place of ribbon. He'd left long lengths to snake out of the centre of each cross, ready to be attached to Edwina. All done prior to coming to the canal. The less time he spent out here the better, hence not bothering to use the mallet to break the cement and make a grave.

"Best to be prepared, Edwina. Best to be ready."

He reached inside to take each present out one by one, their weight seeming heavier than they had when he'd placed them in the boot. Maybe his arms were tired and it was just an illusion, but goodness, he struggled to carry them over to the canal wall, even though it was only three steps away. Once all six chunks stood in a line, he returned to the boot.

*Now to take Edwina out.*

He couldn't remember the last time she'd left the house. Certainly not in the past week, because she'd spent all her time sitting in that living room chair, not even getting up for a pee-pee or to empty her dirty bowels.

He lugged her over to the presents.

"You bastard," Edwina said. "I'll come back to visit you in your whacky little hospital. Doing this won't get rid of me, you know, Simon."

"There you go, getting all confused yet again. I'm Remington, Edwina. Remington."

"Well, you remind me of Simon," she snapped.

"*You* remind *me* of him. He gave you the same face. Cut to ribbons. He had a good time with your ugly mug, didn't he? Deserved it, didn't you, so I heard?"

She sneered. "I know your kind. If you're anything like Simon, you needed a good wallop or two as you were growing up. Fucking wanker of a kid, Simon was. Horrible little waste of space, always messing up my life."

Remington experienced a surge of sorrow for Simon. No wonder the man had done what he had to Edwina. The woman was pure evil and still couldn't keep her mouth shut even though she was dea—

*She's not dead— how can she be when she's speaking to me? But she won't be speaking for much longer. The canal will soon take care of her.*

Remington placed her down, flush to the wall so the shadows hid her should anyone unexpectedly walk by. Who knew whether an insomniac prowled the canalside every night, or one of those homeless sorts, or Runner might appear again, a live ghost who kept haunting him.

He crouched and, keeping his attention off her stapled face, tied the presents to her. Ankles, wrists, neck, waist. Once he'd finished, he had a thought: *I might not be able to lift her with the added weight.* Frustration and anger at Simon bubbled inside him, and Remington wanted to cry. Yes, cry. Everything in his life seemed so *awkward* at times, as though fate put blocks in his path to test him, to see how he'd cope in moments of adversity.

*Adversity needs to take a running jump. Maybe it will once Edwina's gone.*

He checked the area again, paying particular attention to the other side of the canal where Runner said he'd been.

Okay, he couldn't see everything over there, so if anyone *was* watching he'd never have a clue, but the darkness of the night . . . perhaps it would be enough to shield what he was about to do.

Steeling himself, he took Edwina beneath the armpits and hauled her into a sitting position. The present tied around her neck swung, bashing him on the shin. He held back an outraged burst of sound — couldn't he even do this one simple task without getting hurt? All his life he'd been hurt, always presented with pain.

*No. Not me. Edwina brought Simon pain. I'm new on the scene, a whole different person. I must remember that.*

He got confused sometimes as to who he was. That was what happened when Simon filled his head with horrific stories while Remington tried to blank him out. Things merged, got distorted. You imagined all sorts — and you forgot a lot, too.

He hefted Edwina up, laying her torso and head on the top of the wall. Her legs straddled it, her arms draped either side, the cement presents hanging, and her face pointed towards him. Such an ugly face now, criss-crossed with lacerations, all held together by the silver staples. Prior to her recently decorated skin, she'd been beautiful — to anyone but Simon.

Simon's whispers infiltrated Remington's mind, rebounding in there, bullets unable to find an exit, mangling Remington's thoughts and twisting his point of view. He couldn't remember all of what Simon had said in his instructions, so he took a deep breath in order to concentrate.

"Push the bitch off," Simon had said. "Push her into the filthy water."

"Don't you dare," Edwina said. "You push me in, and I'll—"

"You'll what?" Remington whispered. "You'll do nothing but sink to the bottom where you belong, you spiteful hag." A pause. "Oh my goodness." He shook his head. "All this bickering is quite unnecessary. You should have had this argument before we came here. Now simply isn't a good time. *I'm* the one who can get into trouble for this, not you or Simon, so I'd appreciate it if you stopped shouting now and left me alone. Make too much noise, and someone might come along."

He stared down at Edwina, who glared back at him, her eyes seemingly covered in frost, milky and vague, as though she wanted her gaze to pierce into him, to scar, to hurt, but it wasn't sharp enough to do so.

"This isn't my fault, Edwina," he said. "Your issue is with Simon. Now, do you have any last words?"

Edwina's mouth skewed into an unholy grimace, one Simon said he'd seen countless times. Remington was sad he was seeing it again on his behalf.

"You're a useless, stinking little fucker," Edwina said, her voice just the same as it had been at home. Strident. Full of spite. "I wish you'd died at birth. I *hate* you — but then you know that."

"Yes, Simon knows that." Remington squeezed his chin between thumb and finger. "I might be naive here, but I'd rather hoped you'd feel some remorse. Or at least apologise to Simon via me for what you put him through." He chuckled. "But why on earth would I expect that from you? From what Simon's told me, you're not the most pleasant of people, which is why I agreed to help him. Sorry — it isn't so difficult to say."

"Fuck you, arsehole." Edwina's stare remained fixed.

The woman really didn't have any guilt whatsoever.

*Good grief.*

"Push her," Simon yelled from somewhere in the darkness.

Remington cocked his head, his ear almost touching his shoulder. Simon's memories floated through his mind, a seamless montage.

Punches. Customers. Oh, there were many of those.

Drugs, needles, and fat, homemade cigarettes. What were they called? Spliffs.

The spyhole. In the cupboard door.

Two pairs of legs, Edwina's spread, a customer's between them.

Grunts. Slaps.

Tears. Simon's tears, the Boy so upset.

Then Trevor, Simon's new daddy as Edwina had called him. Except Trevor hadn't liked being called Daddy. No. Just Trevor, you little fucker.

"You, boy. You bastard," Trevor said, appearing beside Remington.

Remington turned to look at him. Trevor was a visitor now, encroaching on Remington's mission, watching, just like he always had with Simon. Trevor's clothes hung on him, the once bulky expanse of his body long gone. Years ago, the man had been so tall and . . . frightening. Remington got the sense that Simon wasn't afraid of Trevor anymore. Not since Trevor's weight had sloughed off him, starved as he'd been in that cupboard.

"What do you want?" Remington asked.

"I always knew you'd end up a bad sort." Trevor sniffed air into one big nostril — cocaine had eaten his septum.

"No, you didn't, because you don't know me," Remington said. "Like Edwina, you've mixed me up with Simon." He snorted. "And as for being a bad sort. Pot calling the kettle black, anyone?"

"If I had a kettle now . . ." Trevor's face screwed up.

"Yes, yes, I know. You'd pour boiling water on Simon again. Heard this story a million times already. Next you'll be telling me how the skin on his arm fell off, and later, Simon was left with hideous scars. It's all very monotonous, this rehashing of the past." Remington sniffed. "Now, why don't you tootle along and mind your own business?"

Trevor vanished, and Remington turned his attention to Edwina.

"It's time for you to leave," he said. "I suspect you'll become a visitor, but that's fine. I fully envisage you returning, trying to torment me and Simon. What you've failed to realise so far is that Simon no longer lives at the hospital house, so returning won't be of benefit to you if you want to upset him."

He slid his hands under her back and, with all his strength, shoved her off the ledge. As she fell, he peered over. The presents hung from the ropes, perfectly straight beneath her. They hit the water before she did, then she slapped against the surface, her body shrouded by a wall of mud-coloured water. It collapsed over her, rendering her almost invisible, then the canal swallowed her whole.

Remington stood for a long while, thinking nothing, just staring at the surface. Perhaps he expected her to rise, to float, bobbing away with the current for some nosy parker to find. She didn't. He kept watch for more than an hour, stupefied, unable to move.

"The sun will be up soon," Simon said from behind him.

"It will." Remington blinked, casting is gaze at the sky. Why was Simon here? If Remington was meant to be doing the jobs so Simon didn't get in trouble, why had he turned up?

Remington walked back to his car, telling Simon, wherever he was, that he wasn't giving him a lift. If they were seen together, the poo would hit the fan. In the driver's seat, he reached over to the glove box. He rummaged around inside it, finding what he sought. A pay-as-you-go mobile, one of several he'd bought, along with a fair few SIMs.

He dialled. Ringing entered his ear and sent a chill through him.

"Oh, good early morning to you, lady," he said. "Wake you, did I? Oh well. Chop-chop, get into the land of the living." He laughed at the irony of his joke. Such a cracker.

He ended the call and rang a different number to really put the cat amongst the pigeons. "Hello, Mike. Please don't interrupt me — I know you were going to. Now then. I promised I'd telephone when I had news, so here it is. She's a little cold and wet at the moment and can't come to the phone, but she sends her regards. Always did like screwing the police, that one — they paid more for her to keep their visits quiet. Perhaps you'll meet her one day, although I sincerely hope you don't. She isn't a nice person. But if you and Bethany are as good as it seems, you *will* meet her. And may God help you when you do. She's . . . ugly."

# CHAPTER ELEVEN

Mike narrowed his eyes, the phone pressed to his ear. He looked at Bethany and nodded —*yes, it's him on the phone.* She shoved the blanket off her, the one he'd given her to sleep under on his sofa, eyes wide, heart thudding. She'd just taken a call from the Creep, and now he was ringing Mike?

She gestured for him to put the call on speaker. He did so.

"What do you want?" Mike asked him.

A pause, then, "Where is Bethany?"

Mike sat up straight. "None of your business. She's got an alarm that rings directly to the station at her house, so don't even bother going there."

Bethany hoped the bloke believed Mike's lie.

"Maybe she's gone back to sleep. Shame, I thought I would have been keeping her up at night, especially after what transpired earlier. Aren't you worried now you know I have your number?"

"Nope, and it's not something *you* should be calling. If you need to get a message to Bethany or myself, you ought to ring the police station and go through them."

"Why would I do that? She's a police officer, same as you. Surely you both should expect to be contacted by any means necessary when someone is reporting a crime. After all, you leave your business cards with victims and the like. They're easy to get hold of."

Bethany stiffened. *Has he been following us? Or did he come into the police station and take our cards off the notice board?*

She felt sick. How many times had she seen him without knowing it over the past few months since he'd started this torment? She could have queued in front of him in Tesco or anything. This fucker had no boundaries.

Mike moved to the edge of the chair and ran a hand through his hair. "A crime you've committed, I suspect."

"You suspect correctly. I realise you're a clever man and didn't need me to spell it out. However, it isn't you I want to speak to. Please pass me to Bethany. I know she's there."

Mike hesitated.

Bethany's heart thudded hard. What, was he watching Mike's house? She prepared herself to act unfazed by his call. "What do you want?"

"Ah, such an impolite way to address someone," the Creep said.

Bethany got up and walked to the window, shifted one curtain across, and placed the phone on the sill. She peered outside. Was he really out there, watching, or was it her imagination and he was just bluffing? "Look, get on with it, will you? Say what you have to say. I don't have time to play games. Do you realise what bloody time it is? Most normal people are sleeping."

"Oh, games can be quite entertaining." Heavy breathing. "As a child, I found playing Scrabble took my mind off many things. You should try it sometime."

Bethany waited for the man to speak.

"So let us play Scrabble now." More heavy breathing. "I'll give you some letters, and you have to make a word out of them."

She moved to the coffee table where Mike's pen and his notebook sat. "Go on."

"Let's see. Which word will give the biggest clue?" A sound like a gust of wind drifted out of the phone. "Hmm. Here's some background. Like I said to Mike, she's wet at the moment and can't come to the phone. Heavy, too, weighed down by gifts."

Bethany frowned. *Gifts?* "Like I just said, go on, get on with it."

"Testy." A chuckle. "All right. Are you ready? Then I shall begin. She'll become a visitor now, so I'll be seeing her again soon, I imagine." The clearing of a throat. "Even if you get to her, she'll still be able to visit me. No matter what you do with her, she'll still go to the hospital."

This bloke was talking in riddles and getting right on Bethany's nerves. Why couldn't he just say what he really meant?

"Anyway, that's enough background." A sigh. "And I'm rather amused about something. You possibly think I'm not clever enough to know that this phone number of mine will be checked, my present location found. That's fine. You may find where I am, but not me, as by the time anyone gets here, I'll be gone. And my current location is another clue when you're privy to it. So, the letters for our game. Think American on this, okay? The correct word will give you an idea of which woman is wet. A little nickname. Here we go. R E N I W E." He laughed. "Or it could refer to one of Mike's body parts." He laughed harder. "Have a good day, woman."

The line went dead.

Bethany scribbled on the notebook. She picked it up as well as the phone, stared at the screen, then gestured for Mike to sit on the sofa with her, tossing the notebook down. She accessed the call log. The last number to come in sat proudly at the top of a list.

"Why the hell does he want me to know where he is?" Bethany asked. "He realises we can find him via this number yet he's okay with that? CCTV alone will show us his car or himself. We can use it to follow him home. I don't understand it."

Mike raised his eyebrows. "Not being rude, but CCTV hardly helped earlier, did it? No one knew where he'd gone after a certain point once he'd caused the accident. His car seemed to just disappear. I reckon the same thing will happen now. He's not a stupid man — he has his bases covered."

"Or he's just damn lucky." Bethany brought up Mike's contact list then prodded an icon next to Ursula Fringwell's name, the nighttime desk sergeant. "I'm so tired of this kind of bullshit."

While Bethany spoke to Ursula about CCTV and running the mobile number through the system, she followed Mike to the kitchen. Coffee wasn't needed to wake them up, and tea never did fix problems, but it'd give them something to do, drinking it.

She ended the call and thought of the man's voice. He'd sounded posh, one of those rich types who went to Eton. Had a privileged upbringing made him think he could do whatever he liked? Seemed so.

Instant coffee made, Mike took both cups into the living room.

Bethany joined him on the sofa, nodding her thanks for the drink. "Ursula is getting the techs to take a look at that phone number, not that it'll do much good. I think the phone or SIM will be dumped. If it's disposed of where this weirdo was when he called, maybe we'll get something to do with the wet woman at the location, but if it isn't . . ." She released a breath. "Wet. Is he being rude, d'you think?"

"Rude?" Seemed Mike had to think for a moment. "Oh . . . I took it literally, that her body is wet, not . . . *that*."

"Well, you just don't know with these people. It could be a sexual abuse case." Bethany closed her eyes briefly. "We may as well go into bloody work now." She glanced up at the wall clock. "Meant to be there in three hours anyway."

Mike shook his head. "No point in me suggesting we try to get a couple more hours of sleep then."

"Will *you* be able to sleep after a phone call like that?" Bethany sipped her coffee. "Jesus Christ, this bloke's mental, got to be."

"Most of them are."

Coffee finished, she set her cup down on the table. Closed her eyes. Let her mind drift. She waited for it to throw stuff at her, scenarios and whatnot. It didn't take long for things to piece together. She thought about the woman — she was wet, so Bethany took it to mean the obvious, like Mike had thought, that she'd been doused in water. But what if it wasn't water? What about petrol? She shuddered at that, hoping the latter wasn't the case. The idea of the man burning her alive had her wincing — especially because right at this moment, there wasn't anything they could do about it. She was unknown to them, a faceless victim of a madman's warped desires.

*As long as I live, I'll never understand people like him.*

She recalled the letters, which she'd memorised.

R E N I W E.

If she said it as a whole word, it sounded similar to 'renew'. Was that what the man meant? Was the woman wet because he'd baptised her in his form of holy water? Did God play a part in this bloke's excuse for why he was behaving as he was? There were too many times to count where people blamed the Big Man for what they'd done. Besides, renew wasn't a word she'd associate with one of Mike's body parts — or at least she couldn't think of how it was significant. And renew wasn't solely an American word either.

She tossed the letters around in her head, coming up with a few words she felt didn't have anything to do with the woman or the case.

Wine. New. Ere. Were. Win.

*What the hell is this man on? Drugs or what?*

As she imagined the letters in a line inside her mind, she continued trying to create more words, coming up blank. The more she concentrated, the more she floated in that state between awake and asleep. Then . . .

WIENER.

"Fuck, yes," she whispered.

Wiener, an American word also used to refer to a body part.

So what did that mean?

# CHAPTER TWELVE

Bethany stood at the head of the incident room.

"As we're all painfully aware, I've been receiving strange phone calls from a gentleman—" she paused while they either snorted or chuckled at her polite term for the man — "for a while. At first, I dismissed him as a crackpot, but during the night, things changed. Not only did he call again, giving me even more of an idea that he's a killer, but as Glen and Mike know, he tried to run me off the road."

"Shit," Leona muttered.

"Shit indeed." Bethany gave a tight smile. She went on to explain how the Creep wanted to play Scrabble and what she thought the word puzzle meant.

"Do you think this Weiner is the Creep?" Fran asked. "I mean, is he calling himself Dick, so his name might be Richard?

"No idea — that's something we need to discover."

"Big operation ahead then." Leona rubbed her forehead.

"Yep, the tedious job of looking through names for any Richards. Did Ursula send either of you an email about the phone he used?"

Glen pushed himself off the right-hand wall and came to stand at the front beside Bethany. "Number's registered as a pay-as-you-go, but we have a general location. Warehouse by the canal."

It seemed as though the whole room groaned.

"Yes, I know, pay-as-you-go phones are a bastard in terms of us knowing who uses them," Bethany said, "but there's always the chance we can find out where it was purchased and who by. Someone needs to check which shop that SIM landed in after delivery from the factory." Bethany shifted her sights around the room. "Fran, you're the best one for this. See if the shop has a record of when it was sold. When you get a time frame, visit the shop and ask to see their CCTV if they have any. You know how it goes." She scratched her head. "We've got lucky in the past on this sort of thing, maybe we will this time, too. It'd be nice to wrap this up pretty quickly."

*But in my experience, no murder case has ever been easy. Always some bollocks in the way, stopping us having a smooth ride.*

"Any news on finding out where the Creep's car went to after CCTV lost track of it?" she asked.

Leona raised her pen. "We've been looking again at all CCTV in the vicinity of where the car vanished. Like the first time we went through it, no luck so far."

"Thank you." Bethany looked at Glen. "You staying with us on this or are you needed elsewhere?"

He nodded. "Thought you might need the help."

Bethany didn't try to dissuade him. "Right. We can't go dragging the whole section of the sodding canal where the location is — budgets and all that. We have to narrow things down. So he was near a warehouse — there are a couple there. We need to know if any houses are around, because houses mean potential witnesses."

"There are three high-rises next to each other in that section," Mike said. "The Heights estate."

"Bloody hell." Bethany hated it there.

"We'll get down to the canal then, shall we?" Mike raised his eyebrows.

Bethany's gut tightened. Would they be lucky enough to have a witness? Then again, the canal was wide in places. It was unlikely a witness could have seen the Creep from such a distance. She had to hope, though — hope was what got her through the hours most days.

She followed Glen out of the station, Mike close behind.

"Are we taking two cars?" Glen asked.

"Might be an idea. If I have things in hand once we get there, you might want to come back and help Fran and Leona." Bethany reached her borrowed pool car and unlocked it.

Glen shrugged. "I'll meet you at the warehouse."

Bethany waved then got into the car. Mike joined her, buckling up in the passenger seat. Resting his head back, he closed his eyes.

Bethany started the car. "I've been thinking a lot lately."

"About?" Mike opened his eyes and turned his head to look across at her.

"Getting out. Leaving." That felt oddly good to say that — and mean it this time.

Mike sat more upright. "No, I don't think you can. I get why you'd want to, but we've spoken about this before. Your job is your life now."

"Yeah, it's a big part of my life, but the main reason I joined up was to help people and to bring about justice. I was meant to go home and forget it after my shift. It was just the way things happened with Vinny that I ended up letting my work rule me, taking up my free time."

"I can't see you doing anything else, though." Mike rested a hand on Bethany's shoulder. "Policing is who you are."

Bethany stopped at a red light, and it reminded her of just before the Creep bashed into her. "Exactly. Policing. I can do that on my own — I don't need a police force behind me."

"What do you mean?"

She glanced across at him and smiled, relieved to be getting her thoughts out of her head. To have made a firm decision. "Private investigating sounds pretty good at the moment." She nodded, convincing herself she was right, and stared at the car ahead. "Plenty of work out there. What d'you reckon?"

Mike let out what could only be a sigh of amazement. "You really have been thinking."

"Hmm. It's the Creep. The whole danger aspect, it being personal."

The light turned to amber then green. She half expected the black BMW to come hurtling into Mike's side so got the car going again, shaking off that thought, the image. They were almost at the warehouse, one abandoned years ago. It used to harbour a thriving business — a carpentry company apparently — but hard times had stepped in, and now the place was rotting away, no one wanting to buy it.

"What I reckon is," Mike said, "you're maybe — *maybe* — at the point in your life where you need to slow things down a bit. You've done well getting on without Vinny, so now you don't need the crutch of work, you're asking yourself: What's next? So taking it easier, doing a bit of PI work . . . yeah, I can see you doing that. But giving up policing full stop? No."

"Slow things down a bit?" Bethany laughed. "Are you saying I'm getting old?"

"Not old exactly, just . . . Fuck, you know where I stand on this. I hate the way this job wrecks you with each case. You've seen more shit in your lifetime than one woman should see. It gets to you — it's a harrowing business, murder."

And that told Bethany a damn sight more than Mike probably realised. Murder was harrowing for him, too. Times had changed — the Creep bringing her and Mike into things . . . Well, that was a step too far. If Bethany continued at this job, she might end up losing Mike to this sicko or another one after him.

"Harrowing indeed," she said. "Which is why I'm going to get out. It'll make a nice change taking on small cases. You know, following cheating husbands and whatever."

"You'd be bored inside a second."

"Maybe, but I'll get used to it."

"Bloody hell, you mean it, don't you?"

Bethany swerved the car into a right turning, the warehouse and Glen's patrol car parked ahead. "Yeah. Wouldn't have mentioned it otherwise, would I?"

"Yep, you would. You've mentioned leaving before. But not with that voice."

Bethany understood what he meant. He'd heard the different tone — the steeliness, the no-nonsense ring.

*I really have had enough of putting myself through this crap.*

But had she had enough of the job itself? *Really* had enough? If she were honest, in some respects, no — she enjoyed the thrill of everyone in the team pulling together, the camaraderie, the catching of the killer. But Mike's wording had been spot on. Harrowing — it was all too distressing and not something a person should deal with for extended periods. She'd seen detectives in the past stay in their role a little too long. They'd ended up bitter, jaded, and in some instances, just as warped as the killers themselves. To catch a killer you had to think like one — it didn't take a genius to work out how that could affect you.

She didn't want to become that person.

"So I'll look into premises. An office." She pulled up beside Glen's car.

"Just you?"

"What, you'd join me, is that what you're saying?" She cut the engine and turned to look at him.

"You'll need an assistant."

"Ah. I see." She smiled. "All right, you're on."

## CHAPTER THIRTEEN

*The summer holiday had been going on for what already seemed like ages. Two weeks of staying at home with Edwina and Trevor. The Boy wasn't sure if he'd make it through the six weeks alive. Edwina's beatings were getting worse, and Trevor had taken to kicking him in the kidneys while he slept. The Boy woke, terrified, Trevor looming over him after the strikes, a shadowy figure full of menace and threats. The cupboard was home more often than not lately, too. He wondered if he'd get to go out and play today while the sun shone and gave the illusion that everything was okay. But no, Edwina had said two customers in particular wanted him there.*

*They were due any minute.*

*The Boy brushed Edwina's hair while she put on some make-up.*

*"Now then, you need to cry harder this time," she said. "Like someone hurt you. Like when Trevor pinched you, only more."*

*He nodded.*

*"They're paying more than the extra for it."*

*The doorbell rang.*

*Edwina jumped. "Shit, my eyeliner's gone all funny. Quickly, go and stand where you usually do."*

*The Boy did as he'd been told, pressing his back to the wall. He felt better if he did that. Walls were important to him. They gave him a sense of stability, even when things were unsteady. The ones in the cupboard were a torture as well as a comfort. This one was his rock while vile things played out in front of him. He was safer there than farther into the room, where sometimes, customers stroked his hand or brushed their fingertips down his wet cheeks.*

*Voices. Two men plus Trevor. Laughter.*

*Footsteps. On the stairs.*

*The Boy shivered.*

*The door opened, and Edwina turned to face it, her tatty old vanity stool creaking. It had a fluffy cover on it, all matted. "Well, hello there."*

*The men came in, their presence changing the air somehow. It was more cloying than usual, thick and clinging to his skin. One of them had a policeman's uniform on, and the Boy got a jolt. Was he here to arrest Edwina? To tell her that what she did to the Boy was wrong? Maybe the social she always talked about would come and take him away, to a safer place, not to the nasty people she said would look after him. Had Mrs Saunders been watching the comings and goings and rung the coppers?*

*Edwina smiled. "Nice to see you again, John."*

*John, the copper, smiled back. "We're wanting to try something new." He nodded at the Boy. "It's getting a bit . . . obvious with the girls at the moment. We decided on a break for a while. People might start asking questions if we don't dial it back a bit."*

*"Who's your friend?" she asked.*

*"Mr Collier."*

*"No first name?" Edwina canted her head.*

*"No." John scowled.*

*Mr Collier came over and crouched in front of the Boy. "Hello. How old are you?"*

*"Seven and a quarter."*

*Mr Collier laughed. "When you get to my age, you don't mention the quarters." He smiled. "I have a daughter round about your age."*

*"What's her name?"*

*"Tracy. She's like you. She does as she's told." Mr Collier paused. "You do do as you're told, don't you?"*

*The Boy nodded.*

*"And you keep secrets?" Mr Collier glared.*

*"Yes."*

*"Of course he bloody does," Edwina said. "Wouldn't use him otherwise, would I? So, what are you after? He just watches and cries. Doesn't participate — just so you know."*

*"That's fine." Mr Collier rose and walked to the bed. "Like John said, we just want a change from girls. The lad watching is a nice introduction to see if we . . . want to go down that road a bit more in the future, with the ring."*

*The ring? What was that?*

*"Right." Edwina stood. "So you'll do me and—"*

*"Yes, we'll do you." John grinned. "From behind so we can watch the boy."*

* * *

*Edwina stood by the boiling kettle. "You need to cry harder next time they visit. Mr Collier said you weren't upset enough, and it cost me a tenner. I'll not be having my pay docked because you can't perform."*

*The Boy stared at the steam coming out of the spout. "Sorry."*

*"You know what happens when you don't work properly, don't you."*

*He nodded, thinking she'd remind him about the cupboard.*

*She lifted the kettle and held it aloft.*

*He screamed when the water hit his arm, his skin burning. He went to clutch it to him, but she snapped a hand out and grabbed his wrist, held his arm out straight and continued to pour in different places.*

*"Crying hard now, aren't you?" she said.*

*He sobbed and screamed.*

*"That's how you need to do it for John and Mr Collier. Exactly like that."*

# CHAPTER FOURTEEN

It was the best of times. With Edwina deposited and out of the way, Remington had had such a feeling of euphoria upon returning to his little hospital without her that he'd almost fainted.

It was the worst of times. He'd had to clean out his car boot, and making sure he'd got rid of every single scrap of evidence had been quite a bind when his body had wanted to give up on him, muscles aching, limbs heavy.

It had sent him into a bad mood, that. More so when he'd got into bed and hadn't been able to settle for the number of images parading through his mind like grinning, proud protestors against sleep. Simon had told him about two men, one called John and the other, Mr Collier. His descriptions of them and what had happened were so vivid, they'd appeared in Remington's head, as if *he'd* been the one to stand against the wall like Victoria did and watch them doing rude things to Edwina. And when she'd burnt Simon with the water . . . What kind of monster was she? It was only fitting she'd ended up in water herself, and probably why Simon had suggested it.

There had been nothing for it but to get up again. Remington had used the vending machine to give himself a quick coffee fix — making it the traditional way, which would take time, brought the risk of Victoria paying him a visit, peeling herself off the wall, something he hadn't wanted to deal with. She didn't like him anywhere near a kettle, and having her probing inside his head to find out how the disposal of Edwina had gone . . . No, absolutely not.

He stood at the back door, staring out at the displaced rubble, the pile somewhat smaller now he'd taken those large chunks away. It looked like Simon's life, that pile, all the pieces of cement, big and small, representing every single slight Simon had suffered. Perhaps, when each life event had been dealt with in the way Simon wanted, Remington could dispose of a piece for every one of those events. Eventually, all the rubble would be gone, leaving only dust that could be swept up quickly and placed in the bin.

*Yes. That's a good idea.*

Simon's memories of Edwina came to mind. She was a right nasty sort, as Simon would say, 'putting it about' another one of his terms. She got paid for doing dirty things with men, and even when Trevor had arrived on the scene, the 'customers' hadn't stopped visiting. If anything, more had arrived. Simon had mentioned the word 'pimp', and Remington knew exactly what one of those was. He knew exactly what Edwina was.

What Edwina *had been*.

"She still is one of those," he murmured. "She's a prostitute in Hell. Her kind will never stop, no matter what." He sipped his coffee.

And there Simon was, out in the garden, standing there in the early morning sunlight, dew from the grass wetting his black shoes and the hems of his tracksuit bottoms. Remington unlocked the door and went outside, walking over to the rubble beside the fence and beckoning Simon to join him. It was best they remained as hidden as they could. No sense in the neighbours either side spotting them from their bedroom windows. Remington and Simon couldn't be seen together — that would just be asking for trouble.

"You should come inside." Remington clutched his plastic coffee cup. "Out here is too exposed."

"I don't want to ever go in there again if I can help it." Simon jerked his head towards The Little Hospital. "I thought you understood that."

"I do, but—" The coffee cup crinkled in Remington's hand, and some liquid spilled over the edge, burning his skin.

Simon grimaced, as if he felt the burn just by memory. "I know you told me not to visit, but I wanted to drop by to let you know I'm grateful for everything you've done and are prepared to do."

"So you should be." Remington kicked a wayward rock. "And seeing as there are a lot of pieces here, there's a lot of things I still need to do."

"What are you on about?"

"The rubble."

"I have no idea what the rubble has to do with anything."

Remington remembered he'd just thought those things regarding the pile, he hadn't actually said it to Simon. "Doesn't matter. I hope you realise that the chances of me getting caught are increasing by the minute."

"You won't get caught. You're too clever."

"Hmm. Maybe."

"Are you having second thoughts, is that it?" Simon scowled, his eyebrows lowering to such a degree his irises all but disappeared as his lids slid downwards.

"No." Remington was uncomfortable. He felt a little out of control, that the tight hold he'd had on his mettle was thinning, blurring.

"I can change things, you know." Simon smiled. "Back to how they were before — before you came into the picture."

"No." Remington reached out and grabbed Simon's wrist. "No, don't do that to me. I like it here, doing what I do." That was a lie, but where else was he supposed to live if Simon chucked him out and moved back in? Remington couldn't handle living with Simon, so he'd have to find somewhere else. *Change the subject.* "How are you coping?"

"In order for me to go away permanently, you have to do what I say. How can I function when my mental attic is still crammed with things from the past? If you get rid of them all, those women, everything will be all right."

That was a good way of looking at it. Too much *stuff* still filled that attic. Remington imagined what it would be like empty, with only a few things stored up there. Simon's mind would be clutter-free, and he could move on in life without any baggage. If it meant Remington had to clear out that attic for him, Simon would leave him alone.

"There's a woman," Simon said. "Uses the number ninety-four bus of a morning. Eight forty-five, gets off four minutes and thirty-four seconds later outside that tanning shop, Golden Glow. You know the one I mean because it's right beside the sandwich place — the one that makes the Chinese chicken baguettes you like so much."

Remington knew all right.

"She looks like Edwina." And with that, Simon disappeared.

Remington was left staring at the spot Simon had been standing on, thinking that if all those pieces of cement represented women who resembled Edwina, he had a lot more work to do than he'd thought. The problem was, could The Little Hospital hold so many returning visitors should they all decide to come back at the same time? Crammed like sardines, they'd be, all squished together, no room to move.

He shuddered. This was unfair, it really was. Simon didn't plan on being at the hospital ever again, yet Remington would have to endure all those visitors for as long as they had a mind to come to see him. Simon would be off wherever he went these days, and Remington would be left with the mess. Again.

"Perhaps I should get on with clearing out the attic in different ways. The cement pile would diminish pretty sharpish then. And it would leave only a few bits that are the women."

He waited for a response from Simon — Remington wouldn't put it past him to be hiding on the other side of the fence in the neighbour's garden. No words came, no whispers in the negative. Remington nodded, his plan set.

He glanced at his watch. It was eight o'clock — he had forty-five minutes before the woman boarded the bus. If he got a move on, he'd be able to park behind the row of shops and wait for her. He couldn't go out the front. The high street might still be relatively empty — people would be taking their kids to school and wouldn't converge on the shopping area until well after nine — but he risked a few others seeing him as they turned up for work, and of course, there was the CCTV, something Simon always failed to consider.

Simon had mentioned the woman before, though. Hadn't he said something about her being the one to open up the shop, and at eight fifty-five she always went out the back to have a cigarette before her working day? Yes, he *had* said those words.

That was that then.

He stared at his cup, a mangled mess, only a small amount of fluid inside. There wasn't time for him to drink another, and that annoyed him. How was he supposed to function without a decent shot of caffeine?

Back inside, he remembered he'd agreed to take Simon's medication for him. Why he'd said yes to that he didn't know, but before he forgot, he dragged the daily pill box across the kitchen worktop towards him. There were seven individual compartments inside. What day was it? He'd lost track, couldn't remember for the life of him, but a tiny voice nagged that he'd forgotten to take the pills yesterday *and* the day before. Simon had said they'd help Remington function better.

"Bugger it," he said.

He scooped out three days' worth of tablets. Held them in his palm. Saw them as the rubble outside. Would that pile ever be cleared? Would he always see things in this way, a mountain that he could never make smaller? Would he always hold rubble in his palm — that rubble being tablets that he'd always have to take if he ended up getting addicted to the bloody things?

He scoffed them dry, crunching down on them and hating the acrid taste. He swallowed, aware that some of the medication had packed into the valleys of his molars. With no time to dig it out or to brush his teeth, he exited via the back door, locked it, then opened the gate. No one appeared to be in the vicinity, so he got into his car, keeping an eye out for any neighbours in their kitchen windows, washing up their breakfast things. He drove out of the street, the drugs calming him, doing good work in giving him a sense of calm and control.

* * *

Marsha Cobbs stepped off the bus and walked up the high street to Golden Glow, her heels clacking on the ground. She had a fair few clients booked in for today. She still couldn't get over how well her business had taken off. Seemed the people of Shadwell liked a good tan — or, as she preferred to peddle it, a healthy skin tone. Marsha also offered facials, plus body moisturising after the customers bad baked on her tanning beds. It was more like a massage really, and some women came in just for that to destress after a hard week at work or to get away from their kids and husbands for an hour or two.

Marsha loved what she did and couldn't imagine doing anything else. When she was older, ready to retire, she already had plans to fly off and live abroad, getting a real tan from Mother Nature's beautiful sun instead of under the UVA light her beds belted out, along with ultraviolet.

Still, there was no time to contemplate her later years now. She had to open up, but first, she'd have her usual cuppa and cigarette.

She nipped down the alley beside the sandwich shop so she could enter hers from the back. It was easier that way — she got to avoid anyone waiting for her to open, which had happened in the past, them wanting to come in early, so she'd had to forfeit her little break on the back doorstep.

A car had parked in front of the opening to her yard, and she frowned, wondering if the moisturiser man's van had broken down and he'd had to use his own vehicle to deliver her stuff. He wasn't due for three quarters of an hour — half nine on the dot he usually turned up.

As she got closer, she got the gist of what was going on. Just some motorist sitting in the driver's side, lost or whatever. He had his phone up to his face so was probably checking a map.

Marsha shrugged and entered the yard, then the shop, disabling the alarm by pressing two-eight-nine-one on the wall pad. In the little kitchenette, she flicked on the kettle and, while it boiled, went into the shop proper and raised the blinds on the windows. She only had her reception desk in this area, plus a couple of sofas and a coffee table with magazines on it for people waiting their turn for a bed. There were four doors off reception, one for massages, the other three for tans. She'd have to man both sides of the business by herself today as the young girl she employed for the front desk wasn't coming in. Said something about having a toothache.

Marsha returned to the kitchenette and made a coffee, then took her cigarettes out of her bag along with a lighter. It was so fab to live the life she did, and she'd be forever grateful to her nan for loaning her the first year's rent on this place.

Today was going to be a good one, she could feel it in her bones.

* * *

On the journey to the tanning shop, Remington had planned how he was going to approach the coming situation. Going through it once wasn't enough, so he'd examined all his options again and, sure that he had every eventuality covered, he'd finished his musings with a giggle.

Round the back of the shop, he'd parked so the side of his car was parallel to the yard entrance. He'd played on his phone until he'd spotted her trotting down the road. She'd frowned as if wondering why he was there, then shrugged and entered her little shop.

It was time for her to come out and have her cigarette.

Out on the pavement, he opened the boot then yanked at one of the wires connected to his brake light. It was simple to pop it back in place later — a quick job that was ideal in these circumstances. He stooped over the boot, making out he was trying to fix the light, taking a quick look at his watch to check it.

Eight fifty-three.

The whine of hinges had his stomach rolling over and his bottom clenching. He peered out of the corner of his eye. She stood on the step, pulling the door closed behind her then leaning her backside on it. Remington's breath caught in his throat. God, yes, she *did* look like Edwina, albeit a younger version. Her hair shone in the sunlight, and she pursed her red lips as she settled the end of a cigarette between them. A scarlet top beneath a black, waist-length cardigan, a black knee-high skirt, black stockings, and red high-heeled shoes created a sight for sore eyes.

"Focus," he whispered, blinking.

"You okay there?" She propped one arm against the doorjamb, sucked on her cigarette, then released a cloudy plume of smoke from the side of her mouth.

"My light appears to be broken." Remington stood upright and abandoned his fake task. "Thankfully, someone let me know while I was at a traffic light. You know, wound down their window and motioned for me to do the same. Leant across a bit to call out. That was nice of them, wasn't it?" He was blathering on, always did to begin with.

"Very nice of them." She took another puff. Blew the smoke out. "Any idea how long you'll be? Only, I have a delivery due, and you're blocking the entrance. Might be an idea to back up a bit so the driver can still get in."

"Good idea, but I'll only be a couple more minutes if I can just get my pinkie finger inside this obstinate area. My others are too big." He pretended to get his finger into the hole. "You couldn't lend me *your* little finger, could you?" He laughed, as though he'd only been joking and that if she didn't want to help him, that would be okay.

It wouldn't be okay.

She hesitated, then, "Um . . . all right then, but I'm no good with cars so . . ."

"It's just a case of you poking the wire into the hole at the back. Two seconds, that's all." He smiled. "I'd be ever so grateful. Then I won't be late for work. I can get there in two minutes."

She stubbed her cigarette out beneath her shoe then tip-tapped her way over. "Makes more sense to have just gone to work and fixed it there, if you ask me."

*But I didn't ask you . . .*

"Indeed," he said, "but there was a policeman in the queue at the traffic light, and I got jittery. You know, with my luck, I'd get pulled over then be *really* late for work."

"I see where you're coming from." She bent over the boot. "Okay, where's this hole?"

"Right" — Remington grabbed a tyre iron to his left then brought it down on the back of her head to create one — "*there.*"

She slumped, the top half of her body in the boot, her lower half dangling, legs bent at the knees, one of her tarty, Edwina-like shoes coming off, her stocking snagging on the rough tarmac. He hauled her slight frame inside, packing her in nicely, then collected her shoe and tossed it in there with her. Her breathing was slow and steady, her eyes closed, so he quickly slotted the light wire in place.

"Oh dear." He looked down at her and shook his head. "That's quite a nasty gash you have on the back of your head there. I'll have to clean the boot yet again." He tied her wrists and ankles with garden twine. Stuffed one of Edwina's old socks into her mouth. "I think I need to take you to the hospital."

# CHAPTER FIFTEEN

Bethany stared across the canal after they'd had a nose around. Nothing seemed out of the ordinary. Another pair of uniforms had turned up, sent by Rob, the daytime front desk sergeant, just in case. She frowned. Were they even in the correct bloody place?

Mike grimaced. "Where are the uniforms who came in that patrol car?" He jerked his thumb at the white vehicle, the stripe down the side lit up in one spot from the bright sun.

Bethany glanced left then right. "Gone for a walk to see if they can find anything."

Voices drifted from the warehouse, the large door wide open and lopsided on its hinges. Someone laughed.

"Or in there," Mike said. "Larking about when they're meant to be working by the sounds of it. At least we can trust Glen to not fuck about."

Bethany made her way to the warehouse door. "Whoever's in there, come out." She poked her head inside, into the dark void immediately in front of her, the shadows not as dense farther back where sun tried to stream in through filthy windows.

Her stomach muscles tightened. Despite the police cars being present, the officers could well have gone farther afield and the people inside the building could be dangerous. Yeah, PI work was definitely something she'd prefer to be doing. Not this . . . this woman in the lion's den business.

She stepped back, and two young lads shuffled out, blond heads down, hands stuffed into tracksuit bottom pockets. They must be about fourteen or fifteen, bored and up to no good, she reckoned, skiving school. Dirt smeared their white T-shirts and the soles of their trainers, and both had wet patches on their trackies, as if they'd been kneeling in water.

"What have you been up to?" Bethany asked.

"None of your fucking business," one kid said.

"I think it *is* my business." She produced her ID.

One of the lads made to run, but Bethany shot her arm out, grabbing his wrist.

"Hold up a second," she said. "A few questions first, before you go gallivanting off."

The boy flicked Bethany's hand off him then stared at her with defiance in his eyes. "I ent done nothing wrong, innit, so you can't put your hands on me, blud."

*Why did kids insist on talking like that these days?*

"You doing nothing wrong is only on your say so." Bethany slid her ID back into her pocket. "And to be honest, my main concern about you being inside there is that it's dangerous. Take my advice and keep away. The place is likely to fall down on you."

The lad shrugged. "Wouldn't bother me, man."

"It would if you were crushed, injured, or killed." She shook her head. "Listen, I have a couple of questions for you, then you can get going."

She stared at the other kid, who appeared scared out of his wits and not in any hurry to act like his friend, who clearly wanted the world to think he was tough.

"Seen any men loitering around here?" Bethany asked him, ignoring the bolshy kid when he snorted.

"Over there, couple of miles along." He pointed. "We were there early hours. He came in a car. Threw something in the canal. Over by the crane there."

*Bloody hell.*

The crane was only just visible on their side of the canal, as were the high-rises, except from this perspective it appeared as though only one high-rise was there. A rush of sensation flowed over her, springing up goosebumps.

"What did the man look like?" she asked.

Both boys shrugged.

"Didn't take much notice," the lairy one said.

"Right, off home with you — or, more importantly, go to school." She walked to her car.

Glen appeared and came over, and she explained what she'd found out.

"I'm going to radio the missing officers, then meet you at the other location." He jerked his head at the kids, who were running away into the building. "And I'll move those two on."

"Cheers, see you there."

Bethany and Mike got in the car, and while she drove, he chatted about the case, trying to work it all out. She pondered on the fact that he was just as bad as her — unable to switch the job off. Would they really be content with smaller cases, the tailing of straying spouses or looking into the whereabouts of missing children, their vanishing put to the back of the police queue once a certain amount of time had passed?

Her phone rang, and she handed it to Mike for him to press the answer button and select the speaker. Glen's name was on the screen.

"Got some news?" she asked him.

"I called in the general area of the crane and got an exact location — Rob hit the jackpot." Glen sounded a little more animated than when she'd just seen him. "You want to head for Junction Road. There's a lane off it that'll take you to the canal's edge. It's walled down there for quite a way, disused area, mainly frequented by crackheads and the like into the late evenings, then deserted thereafter. Ideal spot for body dumping, I'd say."

"Thanks," Bethany said. "And why isn't Rob the one calling me?"

"I said I'd do it. Was I wrong?"

"No, you're all right. Just wondering out loud. See you there."

Mike cut the call. Bethany took them to Junction Road.

The whole area was spotted with piles of rubble.

"Jesus Christ, look at that." She left the car and waited for Mike.

"What the fuck's that smell?" He came to stand beside her.

"It isn't pleasant, is it? We'll have a look around before the other officers get here. I've got some paper booties in the back. Best we put them on. Not sure what the hell we'll be walking on out here." She gagged, the thickness of the scent crawling into her nose and staying there. "Sodding hell, that's strong."

She held the back of her hand against her nostrils and walked to the right a bit. With her attention on the other side of the canal, she stumbled, her foot catching on something. She staggered sideways, flinging out an arm to brace her fall should she go down to the ground. Mike caught her just in time, hauling her back into an upright position.

"The bloody concrete is all broken," Bethany said.

Her foot hurt. She stared down at it. Her gaze shifted, though, some sense or other telling her to look slightly to the left. One of the paving slabs had erupted upwards from the centre, the pieces forming a volcano shape with a crater in the top. A great waft of that smell almost had her backing away, but she went forward then down on one knee. She pulled at her sleeve hem to cover one hand. Knocked a piece of the slab away.

"Oh my fucking God," she whispered, battling the need to heave.

Peering out of the hole at her were two maggot-swarmed eye sockets.

She squatted to reach for a long shard of stone, which she used to shift away some of the rubble covering the face.

Mike sighed. "Bloody hell. The Creep uses this place to get rid of people he's murdered? Did he send us here with the wet reference just so we'd find this?"

"It's also possible we're dealing with two different killers." Bethany stood. Shoved a hand through her hair and studied the crane in an attempt to scour her mind clean of what she'd just seen in that hole. "I mean, look at this place. Deserted. Bloody ideal dumping ground, like Glen said. I doubt there are regular police patrols here, despite it being a druggie hangout at times. We've got too much else going on to be bothered with an area like this." She shook her head. "Think about it. All people have to do is wait for the drug users to bugger off then break and pull up some of these slabs, do a bit of digging, and shove a body in the hole. Cover it up. No one's going to take any notice because, let's face it, the ground is just a load of what looks like rubble spots interspersed with flat concrete."

"There could be numerous bodies then, like he told you," Mike said. "You know that, don't you?"

"I thought the same." She stood beside him but didn't look down at the face. "This is sodding awful, isn't it?"

"It is."

"I'd almost convinced myself he was just some nutter wanting attention. Shit."

"The potential amount of people buried here . . ."

Bethany thought about the task ahead, of how many SOCOs would be needed to painstakingly remove the rubble and slabs after it had been determined with special equipment how many more corpses were under the ground, if any. The Forensics, who would have to check whether there were any DNA samples, clues that would show whether there was one killer for all or several. And ultimately, if they ever found the wiener man, whether they'd been killed by the person who'd murdered the poor soul — or souls — hidden under the slabs.

Mike scratched his head. "I hate to say this, but going by the lumpy protrusions in the rubble, there are about twelve bodies here."

Bethany snapped her head round to gape at him. "You're kidding me. He never said it was that many when he rang. Last he said, he'd killed seven."

"Um, not something I generally like to kid about, you should know that." Mike had his eyes closed, fists stuffed beneath his armpits. He shuddered, swallowed, his Adam's apple shivering under goosebumped skin.

"Sorry." Bethany could have kicked herself. "Need me to stay quiet?"

Mike nodded. "Just until I can get my head around this."

Bethany dared to look at the eye sockets again. Maggots. Had the face recently been uncovered by someone else, or had the killer been hasty, only piling enough rubble on top to make it appear the same as all the other scrubby spots of ground? The fact that maggots were devouring what was left in those eye sockets — had perhaps been eating at the eyes for a day or so already — meant the body was pretty fresh.

Her phone rang with an unknown number on the screen. She nudged Mike. "It's him again." She answered it. "Yep?"

"Eleven," the Creep said. "All women. They look like her. All his victims do."

*Bloody hell . . .*

"I take it you know where we are?" she asked.

"Of course I do. There's a new one, although she isn't dead yet. I took her to The Little Hospital."

"Right, okay, and what's the name of it, please?"

Bethany searched her mind for the smallest hospital in Shadwell. She came up blank as the main one was big, and the others Fran had looked up were more like clinics, none of them little. She'd have to call this unexpected find in — the body, the possibility of others — then this place would be alive with a mass of police, not just her, Mike, Glen, and the other two officers who should have turned up by now but bloody hadn't. Fran could be in charge of finding out which hospital he meant.

"It's actually called TLH: The Little Hospital," the Creep said. "I'm there a lot."

"Okay, never heard of it, but I'll have to take your word for it."

"Have fun looking!" The connection went dead.

Bethany called Kribbs on his direct line and brought him up to speed since she'd seen him last night. "So we have a bigger problem than we first thought regarding the Creep."

"What the hell?" Kribbs said. "You mean to tell me not only do we have a potential body in the canal but near enough a dozen buried?"

"That's right, sir."

"All killed by the Creep, according to him?"

"From what I could gather, yes, but he said 'all *his* victims', so maybe he's not the killer but someone else is?" Bethany knew what was coming next, and she bit her lip.

"We don't have the budget for this."

Bethany closed her eyes. "With all due respect, sir, I don't think the victims thought about police budgets when they were being killed. Or how inconvenient their deaths might be to you, and how you've got to manage the spending costs with regards to their deaths. Or how much manpower will be needed to dig them up and discover who killed them." She should stop talking now, before she said something she might regret. On the other hand . . . "I also don't think they give a monkey's about how this case has been the last straw for me and that once it's completed I'm leaving, because I can't handle this anymore."

*Oh. Shit a brick.*

"What?" Kribbs' breathing was loud and raspy, as though he was having trouble pulling in air.

"You heard me." She'd gone and said it now, hadn't she.

"But what will we do without you? What will *you* do without the rush you get from your job? Honestly, Bethany, this is just not on. And anyway, you've been hinting at this job getting to you for a while now, yet where are you? Standing beside a body in a hole, doing your thing." Kribbs huffed out an uncharacteristic, derisive laugh. "Forgive me for saying you're all hot air."

Had Kribbs had bad news today or something? He wasn't usually such an arsehole.

"And forgive me, sir, for saying you're all bullshit sometimes. Listen to yourself. Yes, I'm standing near a body in the ground — who was a person, for Pete's sake — and all you're bothered about is money and the inconvenience, and trying to convince yourself that I don't mean what I say. I'm telling you, after this case, I'm gone." Bethany didn't give Kribbs enough time to respond. "So, much as I'd prefer to shoot the breeze with you, budget be damned, I need those divers and SOCO to check if there are, in fact, eleven victims buried here."

She cut the call, steaming angry, and paced back and forth, wanting nothing but to run away and not have to deal with this. With each new hint at a victim lately, she found herself struggling emotionally. And it was all right for Kribbs. He didn't have to see the bodies, didn't have to deal with finding their killer, so he wouldn't have to experience soul-crushing emotions himself. Was she being selfish, then, in wanting to leave and pretend dead people didn't exist? Or had she done her part, given as much as she was able, and it was someone else's turn to take over her role?

However she chose to deal with it, that was something for the future. Right now, she had a fuckload of work on her hands, and she was determined to find the Creep and see him brought to justice. The deranged man — and he couldn't be anything else — had brought her and Mike into the equation on a personal level, and *that* had been the true final straw.

*No more putting myself in danger.*

Her phone rang. She glimpsed Kribbs' name on the screen and braced herself for a mouthful from her boss. "Bethany here."

"I've managed to juggle the budget."

*That's good of you . . .*

"And although the divers and the ground team you need won't be as many people as you'd like . . ." Kribbs waffled on.

Bethany only half listened. Kribbs was a good man for the most part, and she understood the pressure he was under, but today she couldn't deal with talk about money.

She wished for some kind of understanding from him, some verbal that would tell her he sympathised with the victims, but none came. Once he'd finished speaking, Bethany just about managed to end the call on a polite note.

Grouchy, she slid her phone into her pocket, getting herself worked up at the fact the other two officers *still* hadn't turned up yet. Didn't anyone understand that the dead woman in the canal could get dislodged at any moment and they'd lose her, possibly for days, weeks, forever? Bethany itched to have her found as soon as possible, to get the poor woman's post-mortem done — providing her body wasn't an overly bloated, unworkable mess — so she could be laid to rest in a respectful way.

She quickly rang Rob about the missing officers in case something untoward had happened, then shoved her phone away again.

She walked over to the canal wall, the paper booties creating scuffing noises on the ground. The water jostled against the brick, jumping up with every mini wave, and somewhere down there, beneath the glossy dark-brown surface, was a body — possibly even more. She needed to get her thoughts in order, otherwise she was in danger of shouting out in anger — or running so fast she'd be away from here in no time.

*Call in the information about The Little Hospital — have Fran do a search on that.*

*Wait for the divers and SOCO to arrive — if they're not here in five minutes, I'm going to blow a gasket.*

*Go crazy inside my head until we get some kind of clue, a break as to who the Creep is.*

She stared at the sky. The burden of finding that new woman alive, the one in his theatre, settled heavier on her shoulders. It was more painful than ever.

*Last case. I mean it. This is the last fucking case.*

## CHAPTER SIXTEEN

*The Boy had to stop himself from scratching his arm. He'd had some Savlon and a bandage thrown at him after Edwina had poured the boiled water, and the Boy had managed to sort it all out by himself. He'd felt like a doctor, fixing a patient, and he wondered whether that was what he'd really be when he was older. Some sort of fluid had seeped through the bandage, reddish at first, then yellow, and it had dried, leaving the material all hard and uncomfortable.*

*He took the bandage off and stared at his arm. The skin had lifted, broken, and some underneath was pink and raw, all the way down his forearm at various points where she'd concentrated the pours on five sites. It hurt, itched even more now the air had got to it.*

*He went to the kitchen and filled the bowl with warm soapy water so he could clean up. There were a few bandages in rolled packages in the first-aid box, so he'd use one of those with more Savlon.*

*Edwina came in, and the Boy jumped, sploshing water on the draining board.*

*"What are you doing?" she asked.*

*"Cleaning my arm." He held it up for her to see.*

*"That's a bit of a mess, isn't it. Good job it's the summer holidays. No one needs to know you hurt yourself. Reckon that'll scar." She nodded at his arm. "So when you go back to school, you tell them you*

*were being a kind, good boy and making your mum a cup of tea, and you spilt the water on yourself."*

*He nodded.*

*"If you tell the truth, I'll get John the policeman here to arrest you for lying."*

*"You lie all the time," he mumbled and faced the sink again.*

*"What was that?" She grabbed his shoulder and swung him around.*

*"I said I lie all the time."*

*"Do you lie to me?" She dug her fingertips in his shoulder.*

*"No."*

*"Do you lie to Trevor?" A harder dig.*

*"No."*

*"Then you don't lie all the time, do you, so that in itself is a lie."*

*He shook his head, gazing up at her as she glared down at him. She reached across, out of his line of sight, then put that arm behind her back.*

*"What happens if you lie to me?" she asked.*

*"You'll hurt me."*

*"Yes, I'll hurt you. But how will I hurt you?"*

*"By smacking me then putting me in the cupboard."*

*"I just thought of a new way to hurt you."*

*His knees buckled.*

*She brought her arm around, swiping her hand in front of his face. He waited for the sting of a punch, the crack of knuckles on bone, but only a strange, hot sensation crept along his cheek, a line of heat from a semi-sharp knife.*

*She stared at him. "Beautiful." A pause. "Here's a few more to match. And they're going to scar, too."*

* * *

*The Boy came to in his bed, Edwina and Trevor standing beside it, staring down at him.*

*"Ah, he's awake," Trevor said. "Don't fucking pass out like that again, kid. You know damn well we don't take you to no doctor if you*

*get hurt." He pointed at the Boy's face. "It's all cleaned and disinfected now, so he's all yours, Wina."*

*To the Boy, it sounded like Trevor had said 'wiener'.*

*He had no time to think about that anymore.*

*Edwina came towards him with a stapler.*

* * *

*The Boy knocked on Mrs Saunders' door a week after the staples came out. Trevor had given him some medicine to make him go to sleep at removal time, and when he'd woken up, all that was left were red lines criss-crossing his cheeks. It was just like he'd been scratched by a cat. While his face had healed, Edwina had thrown disinfectant on the wounds. It had hurt so much he'd cried every time.*

*He wanted a glass of Mrs Saunders' lemonade, or maybe he wanted to tell her what had happened. He wasn't sure, but if he just went inside, her asking questions might steer him in the right direction. He had some questions of his own and hoped she'd answer them — if he had the guts to say them out loud.*

*She pulled the door back and stared. "Oh my bloody good God, what happened to you?"*

*He yanked the story from the back of his mind, the one Edwina had told him to say. "I got my face caught on a barbed wire fence when I was out playing." He shrugged. "It's all better now."*

*She frowned, seemed to ponder something, and his tummy muscles tightened. What was she thinking?*

*"What are those dots?" she asked.*

*She must mean where the staples had gone in.*

*"The ends of the barb bits. The lines are where it scratched me."*

*Would she believe that? Knife slashes were more vicious than barbs. If a doctor saw him, would they know it was a blade that had done it?*

*"Hmm. Okay." She folded her arms. "Want some lemonade?"*

*Once again, he followed her into the kitchen. She had a different flower on the sill, purple, and one crumb in front of the bread bin. He sat at the table, nerves pinching.*

*"What happens when the social take you away?" he blurted.*

*She poured his drink. "They put you into care. Some are put into a big home with lots of other children, and others are placed with foster parents, more like part of a family in a house."*

*"They're the mean ones, so I think I'd want to go into a big home."*

*She placed the glass on a coaster in front of him. "There aren't many mean ones. Most foster parents are lovely and just want to help." She sat opposite. "Why are you asking?"*

*He shrugged. "Dunno."*

*"How do you even know about the social services at your age?"*

*He sipped his drink. "Edwina told me I'd go there if I lied or I wasn't good." But he'd lied about the lines on his face, so would he end up having to go anyway? No, she'd said some lies were allowed, but only the ones she told him to tell.*

*That was okay then. He relaxed a bit.*

*"You don't go there for that." She lit a fag and sucked on it, and the end glowed orange. "You go if you're mistreated at home, or if your parents die and there's no one else to look after you. Things like that."*

*He was mistreated, but his parents weren't dead. Well, Edwina wasn't, but he didn't know about his real dad. And Trevor liked to point out he wasn't his father, so there was only Edwina to think about here. If she died, would he have to stay with Trevor? He was her husband, so . . .*

*He asked Mrs Saunders.*

*"I expect so," she said. "So long as he's kind to you. Is he kind?"*

*The Boy nodded.*

*"Is your mother kind?"*

*He nodded again.*

*"That's good then. If they're not, you will come and tell me, won't you?"*

*"Yeah." He sipped more lemonade.*

*She talked about growing plants then, and he told her they had an indoor garden, then realised, by the look on her face, he shouldn't have said anything. Trevor had warned him that growing stuff indoors wasn't allowed. So why did Mrs Saunders have the yellow pansy and the purple flower then?*

*Things were so confusing.*

*"An indoor garden?" she asked, her expression full of suspicion, like Edwina's usually was. "What sort of indoor garden?"*

*"Like your flowers." He pointed to the windowsill. "Just like those."*

*He'd lied, but it was okay, he couldn't get taken into care for that, Mrs Saunders had said so, and he believed her.*

*"How come so many men turn up at your house?" she asked.*

*"Edwina and Trevor have loads of friends." He let out a little burp. "They have parties, and I cry a lot. I don't like the parties."*

*"Loud music hurts your ears?"*

*There wasn't any music, but he said "Yeah . . ." anyway.*

*She nodded absently. "I'd cry at that, too."*

*"But it's all right, I just stand against the wall."*

*"I see."*

*She didn't, and she never would, and now he knew he wouldn't be snatched away to foster parents for lying or being naughty, his curiosity had been flattened. He'd ask the other questions another time.*

*He could have more lemonade then.*

## CHAPTER SEVENTEEN

Remington circled the tanned woman as she rested naked, still out for the count, on the operating table. This part — well, when she woke up — was the most distasteful bit. Simon had insisted that Remington do this weird ritual whether he liked it or not. And it *was* weird, considering Simon would never come into the hospital and see the fruits of Remington's labours. So what was the point of doing it then? Simon would never know whether Remington did or didn't.

"But he might trick me, come back to the hospital after all, and ask to see the mosaic. If there aren't enough tiles on it, he'll know I didn't do what he told me to."

Life was such a dilemma sometimes. Yes, he had strict instructions and was more than capable now of dealing with women who looked like Edwina — he'd dealt with so many he was an old hand at the job these days. But getting the tiles for the mosaic then doing what he had to do to attach them to the canvas . . . He didn't like that at all. Simon had said that the canvas, once filled with tiles, would make a good picture, something he could study often, make images out of it, whatever that meant.

Remington battled away a heave. Slapped the tanned woman's cheek several times until she woke up, her eyes going wide, her mouth moving beneath the duct tape as she tried to scream. He smiled. It had helped to alleviate some tension, slapping her like that, so that her head swayed from side to side, her hair whipping about, a maelstrom of wavering strands that, to Remington's mind, matched how it would writhe when he placed her in the canal.

"But I don't think I can put you in there now," he said to her. "I've alerted Bethany and Mike as to where Edwina is, so Simon's disposal location is compromised. I don't trust myself going to any other place along the canal."

Wasn't that what he'd secretly, subconsciously planned, though? Secretly, because telling Simon that he'd intentionally given the police clues, therefore narrowing down Remington's options of where to place bodies, wasn't a good idea.

Simon would be cross.

Remington didn't feel the same as he had before. Something was slipping inside his mind. The Remington he'd created wasn't as confident.

*Maybe me taking all those tablets at once has done something to me.*

He gave the woman his attention again. She snorted through her nose. Panicking, she was panicking far too much. She tried to lift her hands and lash out with her legs but failed. He'd strapped her down onto the table, no chance of her being able to get up.

*Such a shame she looks like Edwina. If she didn't, she wouldn't be here.*

A sudden urge to cry took hold of him.

"I want Simon to stop telling me what to do," he whispered into her ear, brushing her lobe with his lips. "I want to be a good boy."

He stroked her cheek, which was red from his battering.

"You understand, don't you, Edwina? I want to be a good boy so you like me — love me. But Simon won't let me. He says I don't need your like or love. He says you don't deserve me wanting to like and love you after all you've done to him."

She narrowed her eyes, this new Edwina, clearly confused as to what he was talking about. If he thought she wouldn't scream the place down, he'd remove the tape from her face and Edwina's sock from her mouth so he could talk to her and make friends. But she'd scream — they all had — and he didn't trust her. No, no one should trust Edwina. Foul-mouthed, cruel Edwina.

He did what Simon would want and stood upright to slap Edwina's cheek again — hard, so very hard. His palm stung, so he rubbed it against his white lab coat. Turning away from her pitiful gaze, he rustled about on his tool trolley and located a surgical mouth mask and a pair of clear plastic goggles. He'd learnt from experience that when collecting the tiles for the canvas, things could get messy. He didn't like the fluid going into his eyes or his mouth, so he put the mask and goggles on, feeling like a proper surgeon once again.

"Now then," he said, voice muffled because of the mask, "I see you have just the right number that I need plus an extra one." He prodded parts of her face one after the other, counting out six jabs then stopping. "This may sting a little."

He selected a scalpel from his trolley and took a moment to close his eyes and meditate. He needed a steady hand. The tiles had to be just right.

*Breathe in through the nose and out through the mouth. Repeat. That's it. Calm. Nice and calm.*

He opened his eyes and moved closer, positioning the scalpel over a mole beneath her right eye. The skin was thinner there, easier to cut, but he needed a layer of fat so that each tile was the same depth. He moved to the next mole — on the cheek, so much better — and rested the scalpel tip against her flesh.

And cut.

Blood beaded then dribbled, thankfully downwards to her jaw so his work area wasn't too messy. She didn't fling her head around. Amazing, that, as some of them had thrashed in quite an unladylike manner, but he reminded himself he'd also taped her head in place this time and given her some of that drug stuff he'd bought from Runner, enough to keep her floppy but awake. He managed to cut the first square tile with her only snorting away like an out-of-breath bull.

"There, you are my best Edwina yet." He placed the tile in a metal kidney-shaped dish on his trolley. An inch-by-inch square with a dot in the middle. "Only four more to go. Do you think you can stay as still as you did the first time?"

She nodded — petrified, he assumed, of what he might do to her if she didn't agree — and Remington smiled at her. A laugh came out of him — even if she hadn't agreed, she had no choice. She was held fast.

*Such a good girl. A good, nice Edwina.*

That gave him pause. Edwina was never nice — unless she wanted something. So what was this Edwina after, eh? What did she have planned in that little skull of hers?

"I do hope you haven't got bad thoughts going through your mind," he said.

She tried to shake her head. Goodness, she really did have such wide eyes, and they showed her fear in a spectacular way, all watery terror and fluttering wet lashes.

He moved to the second mole-tile, astounded by her self-control. She gurgled out her pain, a low rumble in her throat, ceasing all noise once he'd lifted the square of skin from her face. The two spaces on her cheek welled up with blood — such an inconvenience, because he'd have to use a swab to soak it up. He pressed cotton wool balls into the squares to staunch any further flow.

"Three more to go," he said, a cheerful note to his voice. And he had every right to be cheerful. This was going much easier than the others — perhaps this Edwina respected him, understood what he was doing. He'd heard that some people just knew things without being told or explained to. Yes, she understood completely. He could tell by the way she closed her eyes and splayed her hands out on the table.

He went to work until all five tiles were in the metal dish.

"And this operation is complete. Simon will be pleased at how many squares I have from all of you now. He told me once about squares like these. They're from wallpaper in a cupboard he was locked in."

She whimpered.

"I do have another op I perform with each patient. Would you like me to get it over with now or would you prefer to spend some time in recovery?"

She mumbled something, the words distorted by the tape and sock, and he realised he'd asked her two questions and she couldn't respond.

"Now?" he asked.

She nodded.

Ah, what a delightful woman — and strong, too, being able to endure more so soon. It must be strange to feel hurt but be unable to move your body to get away from the source of pain.

"I told you before that it would sting. Unfortunately, this time it will jolly well *hurt*."

Before she could give any kind of response, he slashed at her face with the scalpel, whipping it back and forth, a frenzied attack he didn't enjoy. It was supposed to be a calming event, making her beautiful, but each time he did this he went a little overboard. He didn't mean to, and didn't understand what came over him at this point in the proceedings, but it was like he wanted to obliterate Edwina's face on Simon's behalf.

Simon knew how it felt to have that blade devouring his skin, the hot pain, the shock and horror that such a thing was being done to him.

She was screaming under that tape just like Simon must have done, unable to catch a good breath through her nose owing to her nostrils clamping shut in her terror. She bucked, her back leaving the table, her chest jutting upwards as though she was offering her breasts to him. Sickened by her brazen behaviour, because it really wasn't on, he slashed some more for good measure, to teach her that being sexual with him wasn't something he desired.

Being sexual with Edwina was *not* what should happen.

Covered in blood spatters, his sight partially marred by red drizzles on his goggles, he turned from her, shutting out her silly noises, dropping the scalpel onto the used tool tray. He took the metal dish of tiles and placed them next to the small sink, where he washed each one then put them skin-side down on a sheet of greaseproof paper so they could dry out. Next, he removed the goggles and the mask to cleanse his hands, his face, all the while vaguely aware of Edwina making as much racket as she was able to behind him. He drowned her out by humming the theme tune to *Casualty*.

After disposing of the mask in a hazardous waste bin, complete with yellow bag and a sticker on the top warning other staff not to use it for anything else, he left the operating theatre and headed downstairs for a coffee. Edwina would probably wear herself out soon and fall into a fitful, or perhaps a deep sleep, and once she was away with the fairies, Remington would clean her mucky face and inspect his handwork. He'd been instructed by Simon to cut as much skin as possible. Ribbons, he'd said, the strips of flesh remaining must resemble ribbons.

Remington hadn't asked what the ribbons meant to Simon — there had been rope ribbons on the cement gifts, too. Remington had an idea that if he became aware of their significance, it might bring on more emotional turmoil than he could handle.

*Best to remain in the dark on that one, the same with using the staples. Why cut the women if I'm only then going to put them back together?*

Down in the kitchen, he wasn't surprised to find Victoria hovering by the vending machine.

"I'm tired," he told her. "I've just done two operations and don't have the mental energy to deal with any of your questions at this time. Please leave the room or go and stand in your usual spot."

For once, Victoria immediately did as she'd been told. She pushed herself against the wall, becoming the drawing he'd created so long ago. He liked her that way — she couldn't speak or poke her nose in. And she couldn't get into his mind and start planting the seeds of guilt. And the seeds of him admitting that he wasn't—

He jabbed a finger on the vending machine, selecting the button for coffee. He drank it and worked out the next step so he wouldn't mess anything up.

Ready to move on with Simon's plan, he took a pay-as-you-go phone, already fully charged, out of his store cupboard, put in a new SIM, and switched it on. The call would have to be brief, the SIM tossed away once he'd used it. That would mean another trip out in the car, but that was okay. He could do with a little break. Maybe he could go and spy on Bethany again for a while, although going to her house was off the table now the police patrolled her street regularly.

He dialled her number from memory.

"DI Bethany Smith," the detective barked.

"Oh dear, good lady, you sound rather rattled." The *real* Remington side of himself surged to the fore, the confident, assured Remington he became when dealing with her. If only he could be that way all the time.

"Rattled? Me? Far from it," Bethany said.

This detective was a difficult one to upset. What was it about the woman that meant she seemed poised at all times — except where Mike was concerned? A tough nut to crack, so Simon would say.

"Surely you jest." Remington was conscious of the time, the length of the call. He'd made mistakes in the past, staying on for too long, and he'd used the same SIM on a few occasions, which was silly. He knew better these days, although a whisper in his ear said he shouldn't be phoning her from the hospital. "Anyway, now is not the moment to have a companionable chat. I have to ask, where are you?"

"At the location where you put the woman in the canal."

Remington laughed but kept it short. "Oh, how delightfully funny. Have you found anything useful yet?"

"We have indeed. It won't be long before I'm knocking on the door of The Little Hospital and rescuing the woman you currently have there."

*How on earth has she found me so quickly? Has she got a trace on her phone? And they're aware the new Edwina has gone missing already? Did I ring her to tell her that? Or was it Simon — did I even speak to him since he was in the garden?*

Remington swallowed down his fear. He couldn't bloody remember. It had to be the tablets messing with his head. Much like he messed with Bethany's.

"We've most likely found another of your victims, too," she said.

*Another? One of the visitors?* "And who might that be?"

"A woman buried under some rubble — yes, we got there in the end. We fully expect the others you've ditched here to start appearing very soon, too, revealing everything about you."

They'd discovered the other visitors? Good grief . . . He vaguely remembered phoning her to say there were eleven. His heart rate went a little crazy, jitterbugging to the tune of terror. "I see. You've been quite the busy bee then." Thank goodness his voice had remained steady.

"As have you."

"Moving swiftly along . . . I wanted to let you know that the tanned woman I currently have will not be disposed of where you are, obviously. I have a little clue for you." He paused for dramatic effect. "Incineration. To quote the dictionary: 'The destruction of something, especially waste material, by burning.' She is a waste — of time and space. She is actual waste — rubbish. Goodbye, Detective."

Remington ended the call then rushed upstairs to check on the new Edwina. She was asleep, but just to be sure she'd remain that way, he ripped the tape off her mouth, removed the sock, and poured the date-rape drug in. Replacing the sock and tape, he left her to her dreams, stripping off his lab coat then locking the house. He sped off in his car, eager to catch a glimpse of Bethany and Mike at work. He ditched the SIM out of the window along the route. Once there, at a hidden spot a safe distance away, his car hidden, too, his binoculars all but glued to his face, he decided to have a chat with Simon, give him a ring on his normal phone. Things were progressing far too quickly, and with Bethany's mention of his little hospital, Remington's days — maybe hours — were numbered.

"Think about it," Simon said. "If they knew where the hospital was, they'd have been there long ago. Relax, you're doing so well. We really don't need you to mess up."

"I won't mess up."

"I did wonder whether you would or not for a moment back there in the operating theatre." Simon pursed his lips.

"What do you mean? Did you come in and spy on me? I know you told me you spied on Trevor in the cupboard, but really, to do it to me?"

"Let's just say I'm glad you came to your senses about the tiles. And yes, I *would* know if you didn't cut them from her face. I can count, you know."

Remington chose not to reply. It was best that way.

# CHAPTER EIGHTEEN

*At thirteen, the Boy had a better inkling of what was right and wrong, so him pushing Trevor into the cupboard and locking the door, well, it was wrong but somehow exactly right. The man was getting what he deserved, a taste of the medicine he'd dished out for years. Maybe if he understood what it was like to be starving, he wouldn't do it to the Boy again.*

*To begin with, before putting Trevor in there, he'd used some of that stuff Trevor sold, shit that put Edwina to sleep when certain customers wanted to have a party with her while she played dead. It had kept Trevor out of it for hours, and whenever the Boy caught wind of movement, he threw in a bottle of water with the gear added to it. Trevor was obviously thick as shit. He drank the water every time, and every time, he flaked out again.*

*That first evening, Edwina had grumbled about Trevor being ages at the shop. She'd asked him to get some wine, and before he'd gone, he'd started on the Boy, giving him lip, a shove or two, a punch. The Boy returned the punch, and Trevor stumbled, whacking his head on the corner of the wainscoting. That was when the drug had been poured into his mouth, while Trevor was out of it.*

*"Is he back yet?" Edwina had shouted later, after the cupboard door was secure.*

*"No."*

*"Fucker."*

*The Boy sat at the dining table decorated with junk, washing, all manner of stuff Edwina never put away. He didn't have to stand by the wall anymore — he wasn't young enough for the customers who'd asked for the Crying Lad, and there was talk of kidnapping a little one and bringing him here, letting him live in the cupboard until it was time to go to work.*

*That was one of the reasons why the Boy had done what he had to Trevor. No other child should go through that. He had to stop Trevor, because if he was dead, Edwina wouldn't kidnap anyone. She didn't have the guts on her own.*

*Three days had passed, and she was going off her head, saying Trevor must have left her, and what was she supposed to do with all the bloody plants? How could she pay the bills if she didn't know how to cultivate it or whatever? The electric had been rigged by him to syphon it off the neighbours, otherwise the energy company would get suspicious if Edwina's usage was sky-high.*

*So much badness going on. So much illegal business.*

*The Boy would go mad from it all if he wasn't careful. Then again, he was already mad. He had to be if he'd locked someone away.*

*Edwina was with a customer now, busy doing the foul things she did, so the Boy was safe to peer through the spyhole. He pushed up out of his seat, hands flat on a few newspapers — the* Sun, *the* Daily Sport, *which had a picture of a woman with her tits out on the front — and walked over to the cupboard door. Leant close, his eye to the spyhole.*

*Trevor had the lantern on, which had had the batteries changed twice already. The Boy had warned him if he wasted them this time, he wouldn't replace them. He didn't have the money to buy any unless he stole it out of Edwina's purse or from the tin, and maybe he would. He fancied sausage and chips from the chippy up the road, and he'd nip in on Mrs Saunders, share them with her. She'd been nice to him over the years, nicer than anyone he'd ever met. He could bring the empty chip papers back and throw them in with Trevor, let him smell the food and cry because he was so fucking hungry.*

*"Water," Trevor croaked.*

*Yeah, he'd get water all right, with the stuff in it.*

*"I'm here, looking through the spyhole. Watching. Checking. Starving. Starving you, letting you know what it's like. Hurts, doesn't it?" The Boy said.*

*"Please, water . . ."*

*The Boy collected the prepared bottle off the table and unlocked the door just enough to chuck it inside. The stench that wafted out churned his stomach — Trevor had made a mess in there, what with being unable to use a toilet. Door slammed shut, key twisted, heart hammering from his fear Trevor would miraculously get up and punch him one, the Boy pocketed the key.*

*So far, since Trevor had disappeared, Edwina hadn't walloped the Boy and told him to go in the cupboard. She'd know Trevor was in there if she insisted on that.*

*He walked out of the dining room and bumped into a bloke who was just leaving.*

*"Ah, it's the Crying Lad, isn't it?" He tucked his shirt into his trousers.*

*"Not anymore."*

*"Shame. I like them your age. I'll let your mum know, eh?" He walked out, shutting the door quietly.*

*"Come and brush my hair," Edwina shouted.*

*The Boy trudged upstairs to her bedroom, the smell in there none too pleasant either, and did as Edwina asked. Mrs Saunders said he could leave home at sixteen if he wanted, and there was nothing anyone could do about it. He'd thought it through, but as long as things remained as they were, with Edwina leaving him alone, he reckoned he could deal with staying.*

*Besides, he had plans for her, to get rid of her as well when the time was right.*

*"That's lovely," she said. "Don't you think my hair's lovely?"*

*"Yes." He didn't. He hated the colour, the length. Hated everything about her.*

*"You'll need to learn how to sort the plants," she said. "I'm going to ask Runner if he can show you, maybe help you out for a bit. If Trevor has sodded off for good, we don't want that stuff going to waste, do we."*

*"No."*

*"He'll be round about midnight to collect the last of the baggies Trevor put together. I've got time between clients to have a chat with him." She grabbed his wrist. "You need to step up to the plate to earn your keep now no one wants you crying."*

*He nodded, keeping it to himself that the man who'd just gone wanted him to work, to cry.*

*The doorbell rang.*

*Edwina smiled. "Go and let him in. It's John next, that copper."*

*The Boy didn't need reminding who John was. He left the room, opening the door for John, who didn't have Mr Collier with him these days, something about him going back to little girls, making money from photography in that ring they'd said about.*

*"Evening, lad," John said.*

*"Hi."*

*"Coming up with me?"*

*"No."*

*"Rightio. Gotta try, haven't you." John tromped upstairs.*

*The Boy went into the living room and looked for the tin. It wasn't on the mantel, so he checked the kitchen. Edwina had hidden it in with the baked beans, in the cupboard over the fridge. He took twenty quid out from the thick roll of notes. He'd buy more batteries so he could watch Trevor suffer.*

*He jogged up the street and, as always, freedom whipped through him when he was outside the house, away from Edwina. He entered the shop and grabbed a packet of batteries, taking them up to the counter. Mr Badesh stood behind it with his brother. The pair of them glared at him. Shit on their shoe, he was, but hey, he was used to them, used to all those who looked at him funny. His scars had faded but were still noticeable. Ugly, not beautiful, like Edwina had said.*

*He paid for the batteries, and the men stayed silent, like it was his fault his mother was a filthy whore. Well, Mr Badesh's brother had no room to talk, seeing as he warmed her bed, the bloody perv.*

*The Boy left the shop and moved on to the chippy. It was sweltering in there, nice compared to the cold nip in the air outside, and he ordered his dinner, albeit a bit late to be having it, but Edwina hadn't cooked.*

*With the hot package in his hands — he'd bought two sausages and an extra-large chips — he walked to Mrs Saunders'. Her light was on at the front, so she was up, but he'd been here this late before. She hadn't minded then, so he reckoned it would be okay now.*

*"Ah," she said, opening the door, "it's you. Come on in. Something smells good."*

*He almost said, "Much better than Trevor at any rate!" but instead went with, "I've got enough to share, if you like."*

*In the kitchen, plates filled with food and lemonade poured, they got to it, eating, talking between mouthfuls. He wished she were his mum, and she'd said once before she wished she was, too. She'd been unable to have kids of her own, and her husband was dead.*

*Life wasn't fair sometimes.*

*"Trevor has left her," he said once he'd emptied his plate, unable to utter the word 'Mum'.*

*"Oh. How do you feel about that?"*

*She always asked how he felt, like she gave a shit, and he had a feeling she really did.*

*He shrugged. "It's better without him."*

*"Thought it might be." She leant forward, her hair almost swishing over the salt left on her plate. "I heard he's . . . well, let's just say he probably left because coppers will be coming soon on a drug raid. I heard it through a police friend of mine. Is that true? Are there drugs?"*

*He ignored her question. "Does that mean, if Trevor isn't there, they'll do Edwina for it instead?"*

*"So there are drugs. Right. And I'm not sure. If Trevor has been growing in that indoor garden you once told me about, then your mother must know it's there, surely. Probably best to get rid of all those plants if you want her to stick around."*

*He didn't know what he wanted. If she was nicked, he'd be put into care, seeing as he was only thirteen. And if the coppers came, they'd find Trevor in the cupboard, and that'd create a right old mess.*

*"I have to go." He stood quickly, downed his lemonade, then rushed out into the street.*

*He ran home, bursting inside, barrelling into John in the hallway, who must have stayed longer than usual.*

*"Ay up, lad, watch yourself." John straightened his uniform jacket. "Anyone asks, I was here checking the house, right?"*

*The Boy nodded. "What for? Just so I know."*

"Drugs."

"Right."

"Get rid of the plants. I've told Edwina the same. Someone else will also come round to check." John walked out, the dodgy bastard, glancing left and right along the street.

The Boy shut the door and turned to walk up the hallway, banging straight into Edwina. "John said—"

"I know what he fucking said. It was you, wasn't it, telling someone about the weed." She poked his chest.

"Nope, wasn't me, but someone knew about it."

"Who? You been blabbing?"

"No."

"Good job we know John, eh? He gave me a warning. They'll be here in the morning. Shit." She stomped off to the kitchen, her hair a tangled mess at the back. "Get Runner round here," she called. "Now. He can sort the shit upstairs then get rid of it when it gets darker."

It was already dark, but maybe she didn't know what time it was, her evening spent being busy. He didn't answer and went into the dining room, peering through the spyhole. The lantern flickered. Probably the batteries on their way out. Good job he'd brought some then. He opened the door, a daring thing to do with Edwina downstairs, and grabbed the lantern off the wall. Locking up again, he sat at the table and sorted the light.

Edwina appeared. "What are you up to? Bloody hell, it stinks in here. You been letting one off?"

He jumped and hid the lantern on his lap. "Um, yeah. Sorry. And I was thinking of tidying up, you know, for when the coppers come here."

She nodded. "Best you get on with it then, but ring that bloody Runner first."

She flounced out, and he put the lantern back in the cupboard, holding his breath so he didn't smell Trevor. Another week or so, and he'd be dead.

After the Boy phoned Runner, he cleared the mess in the room, all the while thinking about how he'd get rid of Trevor. He couldn't leave him in there, he'd smell even worse after he'd snuffed it, so he had to make a plan.

*Where would he take him? How would he get him there?*

*Runner turned up, and the Boy collared him in the hallway.*

*"Edwina needs you to get rid of the plants. Now."*

*Runner nodded. "Handy I brought the van and not my car then, eh?"*

*"She doesn't know how much there is, if you catch my drift, never goes in the room, so keep half of it as payment for something."*

*"Payment for what?"*

*"Dumping a dead body." He held his breath. Had he really said that out loud?*

*Runner laughed, throwing his head back. "You what?"*

*"I'm serious."*

*The drug bloke sighed. "Fucking hell. Right, well, I can't carry it on my own."*

*"I'll help you. I want it in the canal."*

*"Is it dead already?"*

*"No, give it a week."*

*Runner shook his head. "Who'd have thought it. Thirteen years old and a killer. Fuck me sideways."*

*"Not a killer yet," he muttered.*

*"Christ." Runner shook his head and walked off upstairs.*

*It was sorted then. Help.*

*The Boy smiled. Things were going his way at last.*

# CHAPTER NINETEEN

The site swarmed with police. Bethany kept out of the way as much as she could, observing how SOCO worked. They'd been here for hours now with no sign of anyone being found in the canal. The rubble area covering the latest body had been cordoned off with tape, and officers in full protective gear painstakingly removed debris then bagged it. To her left, divers were in the canal, two of them.

Bethany walked over to chat to a man in charge of the body-seeking equipment. Isabelle, the lead SOCO, was getting a tent put up over the hole with the eye sockets in it.

"How long do you think it'll take to find them all?" Bethany asked.

"Hard to say, love." The man shrugged.

"Okay, thanks." A rush of goosebumps flooded her skin, and she had that weird sensation — as though she was being watched.

She spun around, but no one was behind her. *Nothing* was behind her except scrubland covered in high, ratty grass, a tree line, a broken wall in the middle of the scrub, and large chunks of concrete that looked like rocks.

She casually walked over to the edge of the scrubland. From the hairs rising on the back of her neck, she understood, without a doubt, that someone was hiding out there. It would be easy to conceal oneself, what with the density of the dried grass.

As though looking into the distance and thinking, should she be observed, she strained her ears for any sign of movement. Of course, if the Creep were the one watching, and he'd cottoned on to her knowing he was around, he'd bloody well keep still and wait for her to fuck off again. The noise the police were making — their chatter, the scuff of their bootied feet on the ground, the shouts to the divers — drowned out any sounds he might make.

*I know you're out there.*

A shiver of apprehension rippled down her spine. Danger lurked in that direction, yet at the same time, if the Creep *was* there, she could maybe tackle him and the search for the killer would be over.

Her phone jangled in her pocket, startling the shit out of her. She took it out then glanced at the screen. Mike.

"Yeah?" She strolled away from the edge of the scrubland. If she was being observed — *no 'if' about it, he's watching us all* — then hopefully she'd come off as nonchalant. Nothing to write home about.

"What's going on?" Mike asked. "What are you doing over there by yourself?"

She glanced to where Mike stood, beside the body-seeking equipment. "Let me just move somewhere quieter." She said it loudly — possibly too loudly. Forced loudly. She walked a little faster, towards the canal wall but away from where the officers were overseeing the divers. She stared into the rippled water. "Someone's watching us," she whispered.

"Speak up?"

"Someone's watching us." She fought the urge to peer back over her shoulder at the scrubland. "Where I was standing when you rang me? There."

"Did you see them?"

"No, I just know they're there." She let out a long breath. "It's the Creep, I'm sure of it."

"Fuck. Right. Don't turn to look at me, okay? I'm going to cut the connection, but keep your phone to your ear so it seems like you're chatting with someone else."

"Okay." Her stomach muscles contracted.

She continued to stare at the water, the waves pronounced as a diver surfaced to her right. A shout went up — "Got something down here!" — and a swarm of officers headed towards the wall. A glut of excitement spread through her belly.

*Bet the bastard's getting a kick out of all this. Or is that fear he's feeling because a body has been found?*

Bethany strode to the dive area. She peered over the wall, remained on the phone, pushing a finger inside her free ear as though the commotion was hindering her ability to hear the pretend telephone conversation.

A tap on her shoulder had her jumping and letting out a grunt of shock. She turned to find Mike standing there, so she mimicked ending the call then slid her phone into her pocket.

"Do you think he's still out there?" he asked quietly.

She closed her eyes for a second or two. Sensing. Gauging. "Yes. I can feel him watching."

"Fucker. Come with me."

Mike walked with Bethany towards a couple of uniformed officers.

"When I give you the shout," Mike said to the ginger one of the pair, "alert every spare officer here that they're needed on the scrubland — *don't* look over there now, it'll give away what we're doing. Tell me your name."

"Pritchard, sir."

Mike nodded. "Now, Bethany thinks our man is watching, but I want you—" he pointed at Pritchard — "to act as though nothing much is going on. *Don't* keep glancing over there once we've left the site. *Don't* do anything that will draw attention to the fact that we might be onto him." He rolled his shoulders. "The reason I'm telling you what's going on is because us going to find him without someone else in the know is bloody dangerous and asking for trouble. Been there and done that before."

"Right." Pritchard swallowed, clearly either agitated by fear or excited at the prospect of doing something other than keeping an eye on the current proceedings, bored witless.

"Hopefully, we'll catch the bastard and put an end to this bollocks." Mike patted the other officer on the shoulder, a blond thirtysomething. "Right. You. Play along with me, got it?"

The blond nodded.

"What's your name?" Bethany asked him. There'd been a new influx of officers lately, and it was hard to keep up with who they were.

"Wright."

"Okay." Mike turned to face the team working on the site and cupped his hands around his mouth. "I'm going for refreshments," he shouted. "Ten minutes, then we take a break. Bethany and Wright are with me."

Bethany wondered whether that was a plausible excuse. Who the hell took a break when a body had been found a few minutes ago? Who even *thought* of drinks — unless it was a stiff brandy for the shock — at a time like this?

*I shouldn't question Mike. He knows what he's doing. Here's hoping the Creep's a bit dim, that he's too caught up in the excitement of what's going on to question the lead detective just walking off to get some bloody coffee with her DS and a uniform.*

"Right," was shouted back in various tones.

Mike nodded at Pritchard, then Bethany trailed Mike and Wright to her car. They all got in — Bethany in the back, Mike and Wright in the front — and buckled up.

"Listen." Mike started the engine then drove to the road. "Obviously we're not going anywhere far. I plan to park up then head on foot to where Bethany thinks the Creep's hiding. The bastard's obviously left his car around here somewhere — pretty close yet concealed somehow, I imagine — so while myself and Bethany are looking for him, I want you, Wright, to drive up and down here and find his vehicle. It'll be a black BMW, unless he's got a second car or van." He parked a short distance away from the entrance to the crime scene, around a bend in the road. "Right, this'll do. Looks like I've driven off round the corner. Luckily we have these thick trees all along here so he might not see us approach him."

Bethany got out, and Mike followed suit.

Wright got out, too, then took to the wheel. He opened the driver's-side window. "Won't he know this car is yours and become suspicious if he sees me driving and you two gone?"

Bethany shrugged. "Tough for us if he does, but maybe he'll think we're at some café or other and you're just killing time while you wait for us. Not much else we can do in the circumstances. If he's there, then we have to at least try to catch him. Chances like this don't come along often. Got to grab them while we can. Okay, off you go. If you spot his car, call Pritchard and get him to bring reinforcements to surround the vehicle. If the Creep can't get away in it, all the better for us."

Bethany entered the tree line, Mike keeping by her side. It seemed like a forest, but a slim one, a few trees deep in width. They walked in the direction of the scrubland, and she winced at the noise they created by trampling over the underbrush.

*He's going to hear us.*

Bethany glanced at Mike to get that thought over to him. At the concrete track entrance to the crime scene, they ran across, disguising themselves in the trees on the other side. Footfalls quieter now, Bethany took the lead, listening to her inner voice that guided her to where she thought the Creep was.

Over to the right, the grass was particularly thick. Her instinct was to check there first, but something told her not to bother. Even farther along, a few metres or so, stood the broken wall. It must have belonged to a building at one time and the part still standing had long been forgotten. That was the most probable place for someone to hide out, but also the most obvious.

*No, he's not there. It's too far away from the road, where he's probably left his car.*

The prickle on her neck came again, hot and insistent. She stopped walking, convinced the Creep was close. She came up beside Mike, and he raised his eyebrows in question. Bethany pointed to the broken wall and shook her head, then gestured around them to indicate the watcher was *here*, not *there*. Mike nodded. He looked about quickly, and she could imagine him working out where the hell the bloke was.

A crackle of feet on twigs snapped, and Mike and Bethany both spun round.

No one was there, but Christ, how fucking stupid had they been? Awareness flooded her, rushing through her body, adrenaline following it.

*He's in the fucking tree line!*

She swallowed down fear. Glanced across at Mike, who peered into the area they'd just walked through, one hand raised, finger pointed, as though it would help him locate the Creep. Bethany searched the leaves and branches. Mike did the same. Nothing was out of the ordinary.

*Where the hell are you?*

Another snap of a foot on a twig had Bethany spinning back round. Her eyes widened, and a seemingly long, drawn-out, slow-motion shout of "Over here!" came out of her mouth. And with her legs going to jelly, her heart pumping so fast it hurt her chest, she stared at an arm locked solidly beneath her chin, and she was dragged backwards, heels scuffing up mulch.

# CHAPTER TWENTY

"Hello, Bethany," Remington said in the detective's ear. "So lovely of you to find me, but also . . . inconvenient."

"Get the fuck off her." Mike took a step towards them.

"Ah, ah, ah! Stay where you are." Remington raised his other hand and waggled it. The long-bladed knife seemed heavier than it had earlier, as if the weight of it was made of guilt and remorse.

*No, I mustn't feel guilty. Not now. Not until I've done everything Simon wants.*

Getting rid of Bethany was one of those things on his to-do list — before the clever bitch was given information as to where he lived. The Little Hospital must never be discovered — *never* — as Remington wanted to live a quiet life once his tasks were complete. A life so different from the one Simon had lived so far, where calm reigned and shame wasn't the *soup du jour.*

Remington was pleased to see Mike did as he'd been told. Tugging Bethany backwards again, Remington created a bit more distance, an amount he was comfortable with. Even if Mike lunged forward, it would give Remington time to scoot farther away. That shout Bethany had given, though — "Over here!" — was inconsiderate of her *and* annoying.

Other officers would be here shortly, so he needed to think fast.

"I'm going to take Bethany with me, if you don't mind." He smirked, because if Mike *did* mind, that was just jolly tough titty.

"Nope, I don't mind." Mike didn't take his attention off Remington. "Bethany won't mind either, to be honest. It means she gets to see The Little Hospital, I suspect."

*What? Why doesn't Mike mind if I take Bethany away? I don't understand. If you care for someone, aren't you meant to want to protect them?*

Confusion rattled around in his brain. He fought it, knowing that when he didn't quite 'get' something, it messed with his thought processes, and he really didn't need that right at this moment.

*I must stay sharp. I need Simon's help. For goodness' sake, I can't keep doing this side of things by myself.*

Remington's usual confidence when dealing with Bethany was clearly deserting him. He maintained an outward coolness — although how he managed it he had no idea — and continued to seem as though his feathers hadn't been violently ruffled.

"Yes, she'll see the hospital." Remington backed away some more.

Bethany wasn't struggling, and that bothered him. The woman was supposed to fight him, to make sure she wasn't taken off anywhere. Remington had prepared himself for that eventuality, and now that it wasn't happening, his equilibrium was off kilter.

"*And*," Remington said grandly, "she'll get to meet the tanned woman. The new Wiener. Perhaps I'll enlist her help while she's there." He tightened his grip on her. "What do you say to that, Mike, eh? She needs her face made beautiful. Yes, I think I can do that. Simon will—"

"Simon?" Mike asked.

The thunderous sound of running people wormed its way into Remington's ears. He had to get away — with or without Bethany. If he made it back to the hospital alone, he could plan how to capture her another time. But it had to be soon. He couldn't risk them getting any more new information. And who had told them he was hiding out here?

*Edwina — it had to be her, coming back as a visitor.*

*But I wanted Bethany and Mike to get information. I wanted Simon to be caught. So why am I chopping and changing my mind? I don't understand what's happening to me.*

Anger at Simon's mother scoured a wicked hole in Remington's belly. He used the ire to fuel himself and, with one almighty shove, he launched Bethany at Mike. The silly detectives hadn't been prepared for that, and the pair of them went down like sacks of smelly shit. Remington turned and ran, weaving through the trees and out onto the road. He shuddered at his use of Simon's kind of language — a filthy word, shit — focusing on his dislike of it instead of the fact that several policemen, as well as Bethany and Mike, would be pursuing him any second.

He shot across the road, the rustle of undergrowth behind alerting him that he was being followed. If he could just run a bit faster into the opposite tree line, he'd make it to his car. He cursed himself for covering it with camouflage-patterned tarpaulin now. He'd be further hindered in his escape.

*This is just dreadful.*

He sped onwards, scooting around tree trunks, lobbing his knife into a pile of leaves. He spotted the mound that was his getaway vehicle sitting a few metres ahead and reached it quickly, wrenching the tarpaulin as far back as the middle of the roof, then leaping inside. He'd left the door unlocked and the keys in the ignition — he must have had a premonition somewhere along the line that he hadn't fully taken notice of — so speeding off was easy.

*Easy peasy, lemon squeezy.*

Remington giggled maniacally.

Out on the road, he spied Bethany's car coming his way and frowned at how the woman had got to it so fast when he'd seen Mike driving it around the bend in the opposite direction earlier. God, was she some kind of superhero?

Remington put his foot down and leant forward to peer through the windscreen at the other car. The red-headed policeman was in the driving seat, and the officer widened his eyes at the sight of Remington's BMW. Bethany's car swerved, coming to a stop crossways. Remington swerved, too, scooting around it in the nick of time, then gunning it down the road, away from the terrible debacle behind him.

*The net is closing in. I told Simon it would. I warned him this would happen, but he wouldn't listen.*

He made a sharp left, which took him to an area where high-rises were concrete monsters sprouting from the ground, their windows hideous rectangular eyes, dark and ominous. They scared him, bringing on Simon's memories and a time when Simon had been ordered to tag along with Trevor to collect some drugs while Edwina was busy having a party at home.

Remington barrelled along, scrubbing the thoughts from his mind. He needed a clear head as he navigated his way out of the warehouse district and into the residential area beyond. Losing himself in the maze of streets on the Heights, and gratified he seemed to have got away without being pursued, he slowed. He didn't need to be pulled over for speeding, getting caught that way.

He adopted a calm expression which, in turn, settled his nerves, and drove sedately, heading for the hospital.

Once there, he parked on his drive then set about changing his number plates, making sure to switch the first one at the top end of the drive nearest the garden fence so there was less chance of him being seen by any neighbours. Next, he turned the car around and backed it onto the drive, then changed the second plate. He really did need to arrange for the vehicle to be spray-painted yet another colour, but maybe that was asking for trouble. The police knew what he drove because he'd bashed into Bethany so recently, and they definitely did now if the red-haired officer had done his job and clocked the make.

*But this is registered as red, not black, so maybe . . .*

*I've made a pig's ear of things, haven't I?*

If Remington took his to a garage, and the police had sent out one of those BOLO things to all the mechanics in the area, he was in poop.

*I'll have to spray it myself as soon as possible, when it's dark.*

He sighed at the thought of yet another sleepless night then reminded himself he would undoubtedly have gone out in the wee hours anyway. The new Edwina needed disposing of, and he'd rather get that done and out of the way so he could move on to the next mission that Simon wanted him on.

*I'm so tired.*

He walked into the hospital via the back door, greeted by Victoria, who stood beside the vending machine, hands on hips, a pout of disgust twisting her fleshy lips.

He locked the door. "Really, Victoria? Not. Now."

She didn't go over to her wall and turn herself into a drawing, and that infuriated him yet had him wanting to cry in frustration at the same time. He nudged her out of the way with his elbow so he could select a coffee. While he waited for the machine to do its thing, he also waited for a barrage of verbal from Victoria. It didn't come, and he turned to look at her in surprise.

"Remington, please listen to me for just a second, okay?"

Her quiet voice startled him. It wasn't as shrill or as condescending as it had been in the past. Simon had wanted Victoria silenced because of her strident voice. Remington hadn't much liked it, or her, either, but killing the woman had been unnecessary in Remington's opinion.

"Okay." He took the coffee cup from the slot.

"You've had a shock, I can tell." Victoria stroked his arm.

It seemed . . . sexual. Remington didn't like sexual.

"Take your filthy whore hands off me," he barked.

Victoria widened her eyes but did as he'd ordered. "I'm sorry. I forgot for a moment what happened to Simon as a child. I won't touch you like that again. Look, I understand why you're doing this, why you've done what you have, I really do, but isn't it time to stop now? You were almost caught today."

"I got away, so there." He poked his tongue out.

She shook her head. "I know Simon. And Simon isn't a nice person anymore. He was once, when he was innocent and a child, but his childhood ruined him, and he wasn't able to get over it, put it behind him, and move on. Unfortunately, it's soured him, and he's using you to do his dirty work for him. Did he tell you he thinks of himself as the Boy so he can disassociate? Simon's good at that, disassociating. You know this, don't you." She smiled, probably to take the sting of her words away.

The truth, it stung.

"But you're so much *better* than Simon, Remington. You're a good man, forced to do what he wants through fear. I'd hate for you to be ruined, too, tainted by him."

"Okay," he mumbled.

"Are you remembering to take his tablets properly?"

Remington frowned. "Mmm."

That was the trouble with speaking to Victoria. She knew things, knew how to get inside his head. She'd been intent on making Simon better so he could live a decent, peaceful life. Just like Remington wanted. But Simon wouldn't allow it, not until *all* the Edwinas were taken care of.

"There are far too many women who resemble Edwina. Too many pieces of rubble." She looked at him sadly. "You know this could go on for a very long time, don't you?"

Remington nodded. "I don't *want* to keep doing this, but Simon—"

"He'll go away soon. Just take your tablets on time. Every day without fail, not days apart then several pills at once. The detectives might not ever find you if you stop now." She walked towards her wall space. "Think of it this way. If you're caught, you'll be placed in a mental home, like Simon was. You'll take your tablets *every single day*, they'll make sure of that, and your life will be lovely and peaceful, just how you want it. Except" — she pressed her back to the wall — "you'll be living it locked up instead of here, where you'd have your freedom. Is that what you want?"

She merged into the wall, becoming the drawing, leaving him wanting to continue the conversation for once. He went over to her, stood in front of her, and placed his free hand to one side of her black-markered arm.

"Come back here, Victoria. Don't leave me like this."

She didn't reappear as a visitor, and he stared at her features, waiting for them to push themselves out of the wall as skin, forming a real-life person.

"You shouldn't talk to that bitch," Simon said behind him.

Remington whipped round, his plastic coffee cup going flying. "What are you doing here?"

"Good job I am and I listened to that conversation."

"But she's right. She was always right. She helped you, but you killed her. And now she's buried where all those policemen are, and they're going to find me and put me away when it isn't my fault. It's yours!"

Simon pointed to the doorway. "Shut your silly mouth and get up those stairs. There's work to do."

He'd sounded like Edwina, and Remington shuddered.

Remington tromped up the stairs, his whole body weary, his mind just as lethargic. He didn't have the energy to deal with the new Edwina now — or Simon — and just longed to shut everything out. He wanted to take a tablet, but in order to finish what he'd started, he couldn't let any medication pass his lips until the woman on the operating table had been incinerated.

Fatigue gripped him, and instead of going into theatre, he disobeyed Simon and walked right past and went into his bedroom.

Simon shouted at him to "Get the fuck back here!"

Remington drew the cover back then flopped onto the mattress, dragging the quilt over himself and closing his eyes so he wouldn't see his tablets sitting in the other compartmentalised plastic box on the cabinet.

He reached out blindly, feeling for the dummy, then stuck it in his mouth.

*That's Simon's, not mine.*

*So why do I need it?*

# CHAPTER TWENTY-ONE

*It had taken another nine days before Trevor carked it. The Boy had used the library after school the other day and picked a book on death to find out how long starvation took and what he was to expect when removing the body. It'd be heavier than usual, so Runner was right, the Boy would have to help. The librarian had given him a right old funny look while he was reading, as if he were some delinquent who was about to turn into a monster.*

*Too late, he'd harboured a monster inside him from when he was small, and he had to be rotten to deliberately starve someone. He hated the fact he was bad, his core skewered with the lance of evil. He wanted to be a different person, not the Boy, another one, who was good and pure and had never seen the things he had.*

*A copper had come round, as promised, but John was with him. While the other one had searched through the house, Edwina and the Boy had chatted with John in the dining room. The smell was so strong that surely John would get a whiff, but he hadn't seemed to notice, and he didn't check the cupboard or even ask why it had a spyhole in the door.*

*The Boy had all but shat himself, worrying over getting caught, but he'd had the right words sitting on his tongue, ready for if John asked for the key and saw Trevor in there: "It was Edwina, she put him in the cupboard."*

*Those words, though, they weren't needed, and John left with the copper, apologising for any trouble the search may have caused, winking at Edwina as he walked away and got into the patrol car.*

*Now, the Boy sat in the darkened living room, waiting for Runner, who was due at two a.m. Edwina had finished work an hour and a half ago, and after a bath, had changed the sheets then gone to bed, telling him a customer had asked for the Crying Lad, preferred him as a teenager, so the Boy would be working tomorrow night, eight o'clock.*

*It had to be the bloke he'd spoken to that time, the one who'd tucked in his shirt.*

*Headlight beams scarfed across the closed curtains, and he rose to peer outside. Runner's van rolled up alongside the kerb, and the lights went off, as did the engine. The Boy crept to the door and opened it, doing what John usually did, glancing up and down the street. Runner came in, and the Boy showed him into the dining room, closing the door behind them.*

*"Put a fucking light on, will you?" Runner whispered.*

*The Boy flicked the switch, and the bulb flickered then settled.*

*Runner stared around. "Well, where is it?"*

*The Boy went to the cupboard. Unlocked it. Opened the door and stepped back.*

*"Oh, fucking hell, it's Trevor!" Runner walked over and held his nose. "Stinks to high heaven. How long's he been in there?"*

*The Boy shrugged. "A while."*

*"He's shit and pissed everywhere. And you expect me to touch him?"*

*"We could hold his hands and feet."*

*"Not without sodding gloves, we won't. I've got some in the van. Hang on." Runner walked out, closing the door to.*

*What if he didn't come back? What if he drove off and went to the police, telling them Trevor was dead? John wouldn't be able to cover that one up.*

*Runner returned and flung some gloves at the Boy. "Come on, let's get this over with. I hope you're going to help me clean my van out after."*

*They managed to get Trevor into the Transit, and yes, he was heavy. Rigor mortis had been mentioned in that book he'd read, and he'd waited until that passed so Trevor wasn't all stiff and whatever.*

*There was this nasty smell, worse than the dried crap and wee, and he reckoned it was the body fluids seeping out.*

*Van doors secure, the Boy got in the passenger seat, and Runner drove to the canal, by the warehouse where he usually conducted business.*

*"I can keep an eye out then, to see if he floats over the next few days," Runner said.*

*They hefted Trevor out and tossed him over the wall, the body creating an almighty splash, so loud in the quiet of night.*

*"You'd better hope he sinks and doesn't come back up again," Runner muttered. "But at least the water will wash any evidence away if he does pop up again and the coppers get wind of him."*

*The drive back home was quick, and in the darkness, they scrubbed and bleached the back of the van, the Boy checking that no neighbours watched, especially Mrs Saunders. He'd hate to have to lie to her about this. Runner left straight after, with a warning for the Boy to keep his trap shut if he knew what was good for him.*

*The Boy cleaned the cupboard next, heaving and retching, but all of Trevor needed to be gone, not just his body, his clothes Edwina had put out for the bin men the other day, but the residue of liquid and crap as well. Even the lantern got a good wash, as did the wallpaper with its squares and dots. Then he sat in the cupboard, the door closed, and counted as many squares as he could in the lantern light before his eyelids drooped.*

*Trevor was no more. Next up was Edwina, and if the Boy had to wait years for his chance, he would.*

*She wasn't going to get away with what she'd done to him.*

# CHAPTER TWENTY-TWO

Bethany thumped the roof of her pool car, pissed right off that the crazy fucker had got away despite Wright blocking the road. The damn car had met with its maker, cutting out and refusing to start when Wright had made an attempt to follow the Creep. Wright was now back at the crime scene beside the canal, probably giving himself some grief, taking the blame for the car going on the fritz. Patrol cars hadn't arrived here on time either, and although a BOLO was out for the Creep's vehicle, there had been no sighting of it yet.

The shit just kept coming.

"I bet he's at the hospital already," Mike said. "So it has to be pretty close by."

Bethany tunnelled a hand through her hair, her inability to do anything constructive winding her up further. "You know what? I'm finished with this. I've had more than enough today. Bodies bloody everywhere, the killer a foot in front of me, then behind me, and I let him escape *again*, and we're no further forward until Forensics find any DNA evidence. And if the bastard hasn't *left* any DNA, we're back to square one."

Mike scratched his head. "Maybe we should go home. Take a break. There isn't that much we can do here at the moment until we see the results from the CCTV footage of where the Creep went. They're going to be ages digging up the bodies, and you can have a look at the canal woman tomorrow when she's in Presley's morgue. Who knows, we might get lucky and catch what direction the Creep went in on CCTV. Might even lead us right to him."

"Yeah, and pigs might also fly."

She turned at the sound of an engine. A police car rolled up, parking on the edge of the road. PC Nicola Eccles got out, her face the perfect picture of empathy. She strutted towards them, hands out in a what-can-we-do? gesture.

*What can we bloody do, indeed.*

"I just came on shift and heard the news. Got away, didn't he?" Nicola shook her head.

"He was *that* close." Bethany held up her finger and thumb. "But he had hold of me, had a knife."

Mike rubbed his temples. "And, Bethany, before you start, you did the right thing by not struggling, trying to get away, or taking him down. Like you said, the man had a knife, and as *I've* said before, you're not to put yourself in any more danger than you're already in."

It was time for Bethany to shake *her* head. "You were at risk as well. And *that* is another reason why I'm handing in my notice."

"You *what*?" Nicola gaped at her. "You're *leaving*?"

"Too right I am." Bethany grimaced and patted her chest. "This ticker of mine can't handle any more — emotionally, I mean. Once I get back to the station, I'm writing my resignation, seeing this case through to the end, then I'm off."

"Does Kribbs know?" Nicola asked.

"Yep, I told him earlier. He didn't believe me, but whatever." Bethany shrugged. "It's about time you put in for the sergeant's then the detective's exam, isn't it? There'll be a space on the team before you know it."

"I can't believe it," Nicola said. "You're part of the furniture."

"Well, sofa, table, whatever I am, I'm not much use to anyone. I'm a bloody bookshelf with too many volumes on it, and my shelves are bowing under the weight, do you understand what I'm saying?"

Nicola nodded. "Yes, but it's nothing a break won't cure, surely."

Bethany laughed. "A break? What, like the last one we took? We went to Spain and came back to murder. Always, there's murder. And with the Creep being fixated on me for months and now Mike — how long's it going to be before another nutter singles us out and *takes* us out?"

Her voice had almost broken then, and she swallowed the lump of emotion in her throat. Mike reaching out to squeeze her arm didn't help matters either, much as she loved him for caring. She wouldn't have got through losing Vinny without him, so who would she have if Mike was taken away?

No one.

She walked off, staring down the road in the direction the Creep had gone, wondering where the hospital was and how the hell they were going to find it. Find *him*.

She sighed, cheeks inflating with the release of air, and closed her eyes for a moment. The sound of another engine had her snapping them open, though, and she stared at the oncoming recovery lorry. The day had gone from shit to even shittier, and she reckoned Mike's suggestion was the best bet. Go home and forget it until the morning. Isabelle would have it all in hand over by the canal, and finding out the times of death from Presley, the ME, could wait. Bethany already knew those bodies had been put there a while ago. She'd bet the deaths matched the times of the phone calls.

She glanced at her watch. Yep, it was coming to the end of their shift. Normally, she'd stay on, considering someone had been found in the canal, wanting to be there when the corpse was hauled up, discussing the manner of death with Presley, Isabelle providing commentary in the background. But for once Bethany didn't want that. The case would still be there in the morning when she woke up.

Her decision spoke volumes. Her not wanting to be here did, too.

Glen arrived, parking behind Nicola's car. Bethany quickly gave the recovery bloke instructions, then made her way back to Nicola, Glen, and Mike.

"You're leaving?" Glen asked.

Christ, did anyone keep *anything* to themselves these days? Bethany raised her eyebrows at Nicola, who had the grace to blush.

"I reckoned you'd be telling him yourself in a minute anyway," she said.

She'd give her that one. "Yes, I'm leaving. Had enough. But for now I'm going home. I'll give you the rundown of what's been going on here. If you catch the bastard during the night, good for you, but I don't want to hear about it until I walk into the station at eight a.m., all right?"

Bethany went on to pass every bit of information she could remember from the day's events, then said, "So, I'll be calling a taxi to take us to the nick now. I'll pick up yet another bloody pool car, then I'm off."

She jerked her head at Mike and walked away, for the first time in a long while not giving a monkey's chuff what happened regarding the case over the next few hours. All she was interested in was getting the car, letting Fran and Leona know they ought to call it a day, stopping off to pick up a takeaway, and going home with Mike, either to hers or his, it didn't much matter.

She was done. Well and truly done.

* * *

The second pool car was a scabby little number that'd look right at home on the scrap heap. How anyone was meant to drive around in it for long journeys without the wheels and wing mirrors falling off was anyone's guess. Still, it managed to get them from the station to the chippy then home to Bethany's with only a slight protest at the traffic lights, in the form of an alarming squeal when she'd hit the brakes. They'd also stopped off to collect some clothes for Mike — it was decided he'd stay at hers for the time being.

With the remnants of their fish and chips languishing in greasy paper on the coffee table, the scent of vinegar strong in the air, Bethany sat back on the sofa and closed her eyes. Mike was in the shower, and the pitter-patter of water filtering through in her otherwise silent home was a balm to her nerves.

A wave of exhaustion came over her, and she fought against it, wanting to stay awake to spend some quality time with Mike. It seemed that their whole relationship so far had been swamped by crime and never having a minute to themselves as just friends. All right, they *did* get time to themselves, but it wasn't enough, not in Bethany's book anyway. They were best mates and deserved to act as such sometimes. The days all merged into one long stream of death and destruction, the respite in between a few hours of broken sleep and eating.

What kind of life was that?

And was being a private investigator going to be any different?

*Yes, it will. I can choose what cases I want to take on, not have them forced on me because I can't say no.*

If this case got wrapped up quickly, she was going to use her remaining holiday as her notice. Instead of working right up until the last day, she'd lounge about at home instead, *and* get paid for it into the bargain.

*But what if this case drags on? I said I'd keep going until it's over. What if it doesn't get solved? What if we don't find the Creep and I can't bring myself to leave until he's caught? And what will I do in my spare time? Think of Vinny, like Mike said I would? Torment myself with what could have been?*

The idea of properly mourning her late husband had been put off by her throwing herself wholeheartedly into work. It saved her thinking, of truly acknowledging he was gone. She'd grieved a little and worked a lot. Anything to stop herself crying.

*Move on. Switch your thoughts.*

So, what did they have at the moment? They had the make of his car — it was only a matter of time before they hit the jackpot and discovered the name of the owner. All right, it would take time to go through the list of everyone who owned a black BMW, locate them all, then look up their medical details — because whoever owned it was a nutbag for sure and had possibly had hospital care — interview them, then narrow down who the Creep was. And The Little Hospital — it existed somewhere. Fran and Leona had already been working on that lead before they went home, so given time, it would be found.

*Unless the Creep dumps his car, moves away, and sets up elsewhere using another identity . . .*

She got on her own nerves, conjuring up roadblocks. Got on her own nerves by not switching off at the end of a shift. Why did she let things bother her so much? Why did she *care* what happened once she'd put in her required hours?

*Because that's who I am. It's my job.*

Was Mike right? He'd always said detecting was Bethany's life. Did he know her better than she knew herself? Was he just humouring her regarding the PI idea, waiting for her to admit that there was no way, even if she wanted to, that she could walk away from the force?

*No. It's the end of the road for me. I know it is. the Creep has seen to that.*

Still, it would be a wrench on her final day when she visited the station and said goodbye to her colleagues. *If* she bothered going. Why put herself through the torment?

The touch of Mike's hand on her shoulder had Bethany opening her eyes. She glanced up and to the right. He stood there, all wet from his shower, a towel draped around his waist.

"I've left the water running for you," he said.

Bethany gave Mike's hand a squeeze and pushed up off the sofa. "Thanks."

In the bathroom, she stripped off and stood beneath the water, letting the soft stream sluice away the tension in her muscles. Her head cleared, and she looked forward to her bed. Then again, going to sleep meant morning would come quicker, and she was buggered if she wanted that to happen so fast.

# CHAPTER TWENTY-THREE

Remington woke to a room darkened by the onset of night. He glanced at his alarm clock. One in the morning. Gosh, he must have needed the sleep more than he'd thought. His mind was fuzzy, and his head ached. A dry mouth alerted him to the fact that his medication was long overdue — one of the side effects if he didn't take the tablets. He couldn't swallow them until the latest Edwina was in her final resting place, though. But 'final' wasn't the right term, not if the detective found her as he intended. She'd be dumped on a morgue table — well, her ashes would — then maybe her family, if she had any, would be able to give her a burial.

It'd be pointless giving her another cremation, wouldn't it.

He laughed at that, for too long and far too loudly. The neighbours would hear him and bang on the wall if he kept that silly business up.

Sobering himself, he got out of bed, distressed that the clothes he'd had on yesterday still covered him. He didn't like being dirty, not now he could use the washing machine whenever he wanted to and there was no Edwina to make sure he smelled disgusting because she was too lazy to clean.

He contemplated having a shower and putting a fresh outfit on, but there wasn't any point. He'd be getting dirty soon.

In the wet room, he sluiced his face and brushed his teeth, feeling better for that. He entered the theatre, expecting the new Edwina to be asleep. He'd given her enough of that drug to keep her in Nod for quite some time, but there she was, awake, her face and body lit up by the shaft of light from the landing.

She stared at him with those overly wide eyes of hers.

"Oh. I rather thought I was going to have to slap you into the land of the living," he said while standing in the doorway. "No matter. That saves me a distasteful job, doesn't it?"

She nodded. Such a good girl. Which had him wondering again why this Edwina needed disposing of. She clearly wasn't like the real one. The others had been — they'd all displayed some form of Edwinaism.

"Right. Well." He flicked on the light and walked into the room. Shoved his sleeves up his arms, to the elbows so his cuffs wouldn't get messy. "I must clean your cheeks. I do apologise for leaving you so long. I'm afraid I got a little tired, and one thing led to another, and I was fast asleep before I knew it." He stared at her face. "Oh dear. The blood has congealed in all the slashes. Unfortunate."

He turned to the sink. Filled a metal bowl and listened to her breathing. She clearly knew what was coming — the air was rushing out of her nostrils at a rate of knots, he reckoned. Snorting, she was, all bull-like once more and quite despicably mannish.

Once the bowl was half filled, he selected liquid soap, a couple of flannels, and a pristine white towel. It disturbed him that no matter how well he cleaned her, that towel would still end up with bloody streaks on it. What could he do, though? He'd used all the old ones on the real Edwina. And this Edwina had to be freshened up. There was no way he'd allow himself to dispose of anyone without giving them a good scrub first.

He took his things over to the bed and placed them on the trolley. Leaning over her, he worked away, and once he was satisfied he'd cleaned off every bit of dried blood, he set about staunching the flow of the new trickles that had given themselves permission to drip from the wounds now that he'd disturbed them. He growled, frustrated that this happened every time, but continued anyway. He poured disinfectant over the lines then stapled them shut. With petroleum jelly on her cuts, the bleeding stopped.

"There. All sorted. Don't you look nice? And I didn't kill you while doing it this time. My, I *have* progressed." He swept up a hand mirror from one of the lower shelves of the trolley and showed her how gorgeous she was.

Remington waited for the usual muffled shriek, but it didn't happen. Instead, her eyes bunched, as did her wrecked cheeks. She was smiling?

"Oh. You *like* it?"

She nodded.

"I don't like Simon's face. How strange that you don't mind having the same cuts." He bustled about clearing away his things. "The others, they made such a fuss when I tried to make them look good. Of course, I understood why, having heard about Simon going through it. I wonder *why* you like it. Would you care to tell me?"

He stared at her, the now clean bowl dripping washing-up liquid suds from the base onto the floor. Could he trust her not to scream if he removed the sock from her mouth?

"Now, in order for you to tell me, I need to take that away." He gestured to the tape on her lips. "Will you promise to be quiet?"

She nodded.

"Because if you don't, and you wake my neighbours . . . Well, you know what might happen? I'll stab you in the throat."

She swallowed. Shook her head as best she could, what with it being held down.

"Hmm, there's something about you that I trust. And seeing as you trusted me, behind the tanning shop, I shall return the favour."

He ripped the tape off and tugged the sock out, wincing and ready to act immediately if she screamed.

She didn't. Instead, she croaked, "I match you."

Remington was puzzled. Why would she be pleased her face matched his? He didn't have lines on it. Simon did, though. Maybe she was getting confused — Simon had probably come in here while Remington was in bed sucking the dummy. Edwina had told Simon he was an ugly bastard with the scars — uglier than he'd been before, if that were even possible, yet at the same time she said he was beautiful when she'd cut him. Simon had gone to school after the cutting incident, once the summer holidays were over. The slashes were barely healed, although the staples had been removed, and the teacher had stared at him, horrified, further cementing the idea that Simon was truly hideous.

"What on earth happened?" Mrs Robins had asked, hand up to her open mouth.

Simon had shrugged. "Fell forward into some barbed wire when I was playing outside, Miss. Got tangled up. Couldn't get out, and the more I struggled, the worse it got."

"Dear God . . ."

He stared at the new Edwina, trying to make out what she was up to.

*She's doing that thing Simon warned me about. You know, making out she's okay with what I've done so I'll think she's the right one for me — then I won't kill her.*

*Don't be silly. I really think she genuinely likes her face now.*

The new Edwina cleared her throat. Remington sidled over to the sink to get her some water in a plastic cup. He went back to the bed. Stared at her again for a moment. Dipped a cotton ball into the water and squeezed the fluid from it into her mouth, just like doctors and nurses did in real hospitals.

"Thank you," she said.

An ache set up home in his chest.

"I want to keep you," Remington whispered to her.

"Fuck right off," Simon shouted behind him.

Startled that Simon was actually in the room, Remington jumped, and once again, the cup went flying. Water splashed over the new Edwina's face, and she stuck her tongue out to lick the wetness from her skin.

"You are *not* to keep her." Simon strutted over to Remington and shoved his face close to his. He must have a dry mouth the same as Remington — his breath stank of vinegar. "You *will* get rid of her like the others. Edwina can't be trusted. I've told you before what she's like. She can act all nice when she's after something, then, when your guard's down, she goes right back to being a whore and a spiteful cow. This one's no different. So kill her. *Kill. Her.*"

Frightened at the vicious tone Simon used when angry, Remington pounced forward. He shoved the sock back into the tanned woman's mouth and untied her, still wishing he could keep her but knowing he couldn't. His heart hurt from the pain of it all — of having to part ways with her and do what Simon wanted. If Simon would just disappear, Remington could have this lady living with him.

"But we could be happy together."

"Not happening," Simon snarled. "No way."

"I wish I could get rid of you."

"You can't get rid of me," Simon said. "This is my house now Edwina's dead. I'll be taking over the tenancy."

The tanned woman stared up at Remington as if he were mental.

"He's nasty," Remington told her. "Look at his mean face."

He freed her limbs, her head, and hauled her upright on the bed. Yanked her off. She stumbled on unsteady feet — must have been the drug he'd given her still winging through her system.

"Come on, into the shower with you." He led the way. In the wet room, he commanded, "Get on the floor so I can wash you."

*I'm a liar. I'm not going to wash you yet. I'm going to get rid of Simon first.*

"Simon, please," Remington wailed. "Don't make me do this again. She likes me."

The new Edwina did as he'd asked and stared at him with pity in her eyes. Simon grabbed Remington's hand and guided it to the shower switch. Remington turned the water on — it was useless to fight this horrible man — and gazed down as the droplets soaked her. Quickly undressing, he threw his clothes into the far corner. The woman shook, her eyes going wider than ever, and she snorted, playing at being that hideous bull again.

"No," Remington said. "I'm not going to do to you what Edwina did with her customers. Please don't think that."

She visibly relaxed — how could she have thought he'd be *rude* with her?

"Stay there," he said. "I've forgotten something."

*Get up and run, woman! Get out of here while Simon's following me.*

Confused at his thoughts, Remington scooted back into theatre to pick up a scalpel. When he returned to the wet room, she was still there — *oh God, why didn't you do what I said?* — so he sank to his knees and held the weapon high.

"I'm so sorry." Tears coated his face along with the shower water, and snot dribbled from his nose. He let his emotions roam free. "Simon makes me do it. I swear to God, it isn't my choice."

She moved then, darting up onto her elbows then crab-walking on her back until she hit the far wall. Remington followed, blocking her from leaving the designated stabbing area, torn between faking a slip so she could escape and doing what Simon had ordered.

"I know what you're thinking, shitface," Simon said. "And if you do what's been going through your mind, I'll make sure the detectives catch you."

"I *want* them to catch me," Remington admitted — he'd kept that to himself for so long, that now he'd uttered the words he was terrified of the consequences. He brought the scalpel down, burying it in her chest. "Why do you think I keep ringing them?" He wrenched the blade out and stabbed her again — and again and again. "Why" — stab — "do you think" — stab — "that I went to the" — stab — "canal earlier?"

Stab-stab-stab-stab-stab.

She bucked, she gurgled, she flailed.

Blood spurted from her wounds, coating Remington for a moment, then the shower spray magically washed it away. Her legs spasmed, and she arched her back, pale neck exposed.

"Cut that throat of hers," Simon said. "Cut it deep so her head nearly gets chopped off."

Remington sliced her neck. It opened, a gaping dolphin's mouth, fat globules at the seams coated in blood. Remington's stomach revolted and, as usual, he slipped and slid on his knees over to the toilet where he vomited.

He retched, bile stinging the back of his tongue, and retched some more until nothing else came up. He closed his eyes, seeing that poor woman in his head, all butchered and bloody, the wounds on her face nothing compared to those on her body. She'd be a mess when he turned around, even though the water would have been busy cleaning her up while he'd been sick.

"She's gone, Remington."

Simon's voice grated on his nerves.

"Go away. Leave me alone."

"No," Simon said. "Not until you've got rid of her. I'm going to stick around this time. It's clear you can't be trusted anymore."

"I can. I'm just tired, that's all. Let me deal with her by myself so I can burn her." *Then I'll ring the detectives. I need them to come and get me — so I can show them where you are and they can take you away for making me do these horrible things.*

"Did you not hear me before, Remington?" Simon took hold of Remington's hair in his fist. He bent over so yet again his vinegar breath hit Remington's face. "I can tell what you're thinking. I can't believe you have it in your thicko skull to dob me in."

Remington turned to stare at the woman. The wet room floor was stained with diluted blood, as were the walls. Bleach would deal with that, and the thought of that stuff prompted him to shake his head. What on earth had he been considering? Dobbing Simon in? That wasn't even a remote possibility. Good grief, Remington would never do that.

He stood and lifted a large bottle of disinfectant from the cupboard beneath the sink. He unscrewed the lid, and the stench of it further snapped him into line.

"Time to clean you up, Edwina." He marched back to the body. "Then it's getting wrapped up in a rug for you, and I'll take you to the incinerator vessel."

"Good boy," Simon said.

Remington smiled. Yes, he was a good boy.

# CHAPTER TWENTY-FOUR

Bethany woke to the sound of the phone ringing. She jabbed a finger on the accept button and rested her mobile against her ear.

"What?" she said. "I'm sure I said I didn't want to hear from anyone until the morning." *So why have I answered the bloody call? Habit?*

"I'm sure you don't," the Creep said. "But I need to talk to you."

A rush of adrenaline wrenched her out of bed. She sped to the kitchen and closed the door so she didn't disturb Mike. "Go on." She was breathless, her heart skittering.

"Do you have one of those tracing things on your line, Detective?"

"No."

"And is there any way someone else — other than the police and Mike — can find out that I rang you if you don't tell them?"

"No."

"Then I shall proceed. I'm trusting you with my life. That may sound ridiculous, but it's true. This call may take longer than my others, so if you'd allow me to speak without being traced in *any way*, I would appreciate that. I realise asking you to do this is quite rude of me, considering the mess we're in together, but once I've explained, you'll understand. It's imperative that no one else can find out that I've called you, have I made myself clear?"

This request wasn't particularly unusual. Most criminals would want the same thing, but Bethany sensed there was more to this than the Creep getting caught by using his phone.

"Yes, very clear," Bethany said. She sat on the floor. A sheen of sweat coated her upper arms, cold, giving her the shivers.

"I shall begin then." He breathed for what seemed a long time. The exhaled air sounded like a wheeze.

*Is he out of breath? Been running or something?*

"I am being forced to do these things, Detective."

*Here we go. He's going to blame God, or the Devil, or voices.*

"And the person making me kill these people mustn't know I've told you. He'll . . . make me hurt myself if he finds out."

"Hurt yourself?" Bethany frowned. *Is he talking about that man he mentioned at the canal? Simon?*

"Yes. He'll tell me to take my tablets. All of them. In one go. With that vodka Edwina used to guzzle. Or maybe he'll give me a piece of rope to hang myself. There's still rope left from the concrete gifts. In the garden. Beside the rubble. And the rubble doesn't seem to be disappearing no matter how fast I try to get through my to-do list."

*You've got enough rope to hang yourself already, man. And as for rubble . . .*

"Did you cover the bodies at the canal with that same rubble?" Bethany asked. If he did, maybe it would yield some clue as to where it originated, if they were lucky.

"I did not, although that is a very good idea. I shall go home and collect the rest of it then take it back to the tanned woman's incineration. Burn it with her."

Bethany's gut clenched. "There's still time to stop this, you know." Maybe engaging him in conversation would stall him from killing the woman. "You don't have to burn her to death. Take her somewhere safe so I can pick her up. Then go home. Then ring me and let me know where she is."

"Oh, I won't be burning her to death. She's *already* dead."

*Shit.*

Bethany went colder, the hairs all over her body standing on end. Another victim — another needless killing. "I see. How did you kill her?" *Keep him talking, see if he slips up.*

"The same as all the others. I stabbed her, but I didn't mean to. I didn't want to. I just wanted to make them beautiful, but each time I did, the knife slipped, and they died. Victoria said, after I killed the new Edwina, that you would help me if I told you it wasn't my fault. The man making me do this needs to be caught, but I can't tell you where he lives because then he'll know what I've done." He sounded deranged yet at the same time perfectly lucid.

"So how do you propose I catch him then?" Bethany frowned harder. Pops and snaps crackled over the line. *Is that a fire?* Did the Creep know Vinny had died in a fire and he was doing this to torment her? Did he want her to listen to the flames and imagine her husband's body being roasted? "If I don't know who he is, I can't apprehend him. Which means he'll continue to make you do what you're doing. It all depends on you really, doesn't it? How much do you want to stop doing this? That's the question."

"I want it very much." The Creep sniffed. Coughed. "Blasted smoke. It really does do a number on your lungs. But you just don't understand. He might even know what I'm doing now anyway. He can tell what my thoughts are, he said."

*Oh, dear God . . .* "Ah, that's a tricky one for you."

"Simon must be psychic. Yes, that's how he knows. He has powers."

*Simon . . . So it is the same man.* "That's why you need to be careful, I see that now."

"You do?" He came across as a relieved child.

"I do. No wonder you've been worried he might find out you've called me. So what shall we do about it? About arresting him?"

"I don't know. I need to speak to Mike."

*No bloody way.* "Mike is asleep. What do you need to say to him?"

"I need to know how to stop Simon from reading what's inside my head. He's a man, and men know lots of things. He'll have the answer."

Bethany rubbed her forehead. She hoped the lies she was about to tell him worked. Fooling this man might be a difficult feat, but she had to give it a try. "Mike is also psychic, did you know that?" Did that sound real enough? "He shuts his mind off from hearing voices in a unique way. Only the Chosen Ones can do it. I think you're a chosen one. He has a special key — no one else but him can see it — and he locks a door to a room inside his head."

"How wonderful." His voice was shrill, as though he was giddy with excitement. "Where do I get a key like that?"

This man was definitely unhinged. At least Bethany knew what type she was dealing with now. There were killers, then there were mental cases, and this bloke was the latter. All right, once he was arrested he'd spend years in an institution and not prison, but so long as he was locked away, where he went didn't matter.

There would be no more deaths at his hands.

"You make the key yourself," Bethany said, testing his level of insanity. "You imagine it, and there it is, made and ready to be used. The same with the door and the room. Just think of them, and they'll be there. Can you do that now? The sooner you put that nasty man in that room and turn the key, the better."

"Right. I shall make those things, but I'd rather do it while alone. I can't thank you enough for your help. Goodbye."

"Wait!" Bethany shot up off the floor, desperate for him not to hang up.

The Creep was still there, his breathing much steadier now. "Yes?"

"Where is the new Edwina?"

"Oh, silly me. That was one of the main reasons for my call. She's in one of those big ugly wheelie bins. The kind used by supermarkets and restaurants. You know, the green ones that could hold quite a few people. Her body's burning as we speak. It smells. Such a rotten, nasty stench. Melting plastic and barbecued flesh really isn't the best aroma combination."

"And where is that? Where are you? Of course, you have my word that I'll wait for you to leave the area and go home before I come down and collect her." *Bullshit.* Bethany legged it upstairs, intending to dress while still on the phone.

Mike came out of the bathroom, squinting. He must have gone up there while she was in the kitchen. Bethany held her finger to her lips.

"I shall give you some clues," the Creep said. "Not that I don't trust you, because I do now that you've told me about the key and the door and the room. Such a kind thing to have done. Are you ready?"

"Yes." Bethany went into her bedroom, closed the door to, and pulled down her pyjama bottoms one-handed.

"The first site was for the druggies, the others just the same. If you locate the new Edwina, she's burning in the place of his name. You'll have a whale of a time. Goodbye, Detective."

"His name?" Bethany held her breath. *Simon?*

There was no breathing. No crackling of fire. Just silence.

"Fuck it!" she ground out and tossed the phone onto the bed. She shoved her T-shirt over her head, yanked on some jeans, and grabbed her phone again, selecting Ursula's number. "It's me. The Creep rang. Look up all the Simons in Shadwell. Once you have the addresses, do a cross-reference on that name and variants of it as a location, somewhere a body could be offloaded. I'm on my way to the station. We need to think big wheelie bins. The latest victim is burning in one right now, according to him. I heard the fire, but he could be messing with me."

"Jesus Christ . . ." Ursula muttered.

"She's already dead." Bethany shoved her feet into shoes. "The Creep is more than one sandwich short of a picnic. I think the hamper is empty apart from a crust of bread. See you in about fifteen."

She cut the call. "Mike? You still up here?" With no answer, she went downstairs to the living room.

Mike was dressed. "Was it him?"

"Yes." She told him what he'd said. "He reckons we'll have a whale of a time."

"Whalebone's Fish Bar? Round the back of it?"

"Shit, we were only there a few hours ago. I'll ring Ursula again." *What the hell has whalebone got to do with Simon's name?* She phoned the front desk and relayed Mike's guess as to the location where the woman was. Then she phoned Glen and explained she needed him to help her and Mike.

"Meet you there," he said.

"Be careful. The Creep might well still be there, even though he said he was going home. Might be some kind of trap."

"Right. I'll request backup. Catch you soon." Glen ended the call.

"Bloody hope we catch *him* soon," Bethany said to Mike. "Before this maniac Simon gets him to kill someone else."

"There's two of them?" Mike asked.

"Yes." Bethany put her boots on. "According to the Creep, he's being forced to kill people by this Simon fella." She shoved her phone in her pocket and left the living room.

Mike was close behind. He took his jacket off the hook in the hallway and jabbed his arms into the sleeves.

Bethany's phone went off again. "Fran? What are you doing ringing me at this time of night?"

"I couldn't sleep and got to thinking. The woman is tanned, yes? So I just Googled the tanning shops in Shadwell, and there's only one. What if she goes there to get brown and hasn't been on holiday to catch a tan? I tried ringing the owner to ask if she keeps a list of clients, but she didn't answer. Her name's Marsha Cobbs, and she runs the shop in the high street called Golden Glow."

"Right, thanks. Got to go, loads going on. Will explain soon." Bethany called Ursula, wondering if the tanned woman was the actual shop owner. "Me again, sorry. Marsha — the victim's possibly called Marsha Cobbs. Look up the tanning shop called Golden Glow. Check her for a missing person's report. Bye."

She relayed the latest to Mike, who led the way outside. Bethany followed, getting the distinct impression this might well be over soon if the Creep left any clues at the fish and chip shop or, if Marsha was the latest victim, he'd left something of himself behind at either her shop or her house.

She could only hope. Being contacted by him and told what he was doing was unnerving, leaving her more desperate than usual. Not knowing a killer's moves in real time was preferable to knowing.

# CHAPTER TWENTY-FIVE

*That bloody Remington's messed everything up.*

Simon waited for Remington to take his hot coffee from the vending machine slot. Remington did that and walked to look out of the window in the back door. Not that he'd be able to see much — the light in the kitchen prevented any view other than the reflection of the cupboards and himself on the glass.

Before he made his presence known, Simon needed to calm down. He was seething, bloody *seething* at what Remington had done. How *dare* the motherfucker betray him like that? They were meant to be as one, two of a kind, and should stick together through thick and thin. Well, it seemed when things were getting thin, Remington didn't want to stick to anything. Not the to-do list, the rules, nothing.

Remington cried. Simon studied the man's image in the glass. Tears soaked Remington's face, and Simon wasn't sure whether to slap some sense into him or give a bit of sympathy. Simon knew what it felt like to cry that way, all wrenching sobs and shaking shoulders. Edwina had created such upset in his life that he'd cried enough tears to raise the levels of the canal.

*Really? That much?*

But tears never solved anything. Simon had learnt that the hard way. Tears just clogged his nose, got his eyes all red, and gave him hiccoughs. Men had got off on them, handing him money. It didn't fix a damn thing, just like Remington's tears wouldn't.

"You are such a little arsehole, you know that?" Simon said.

Sympathy had gone out of the window then.

Remington spun around, his coffee spraying out to slap on the floor. He was such a clumsy bastard, always spilling his drinks. "Oh God, what are *you* doing here? You said you wouldn't keep coming back to the hospital, but you're here again. Go away!"

"I have to keep coming back because you're not doing your job properly. You did to begin with — that's why I could leave you alone — but lately? Bloody hell, look at the state you're in now."

Remington placed his empty cup on the worktop then fisted his eyes. His chest jerked with one of his sobs.

Oddly, Simon's did the same.

"I'm in a mess because you put me here," Remington said. "I didn't want to do any of it. I want to stop now. There are too many Edwinas out there for me to kill them all like you want."

"They must be eliminated." Simon stared at Remington — hard. "I know what you did." He took a step towards him.

Remington shrank back, pressing himself against the door. "I didn't do anything." He widened his eyes, the whites seeming to shine from the overhead strip light.

"Yes, you did. I know you did." Simon moved closer.

Remington straightened his shoulders, cocking his head as though remembering something. "I'm not scared of you." He smiled with confidence and puffed out his chest. "I have a key and a door now, so you need to come with me so I can show you your new room."

"New room?" Simon's grin hurt his face. "That's all a load of rubbish, what that detective told you." *Take that, shitface.*

"Oh." Remington held his fingertips over his mouth. "Oh no . . ."

"Oh yes." Simon took two more steps and stopped an inch or so away from him. "You told her, didn't you?"

Remington shook his head. "No, I don't know what you're talking about. Come on, let me show you the room. Let me just get you to see it, then everything will be all right. You'll love it in there. I made the walls with padding so there are no hard surfaces, and it's soundproofed, so you can be as noisy as you like. No more worrying about the neighbours."

"I don't want to see it. If I go inside, you'll lock me up. I'm not dim."

"I won't lock it." Remington continued to shake his head. "No, I promise I won't lock it. Honest."

Simon laughed. "Honest? That isn't what you are anymore, is it, Remington? You're a liar — you've been on the phone to that detective and told her all about me, haven't you?"

"I did not!" Remington appeared affronted, shocked that Simon could think such a thing.

Well, Simon knew better. He'd been hiding behind the fish and chip shop, in the shadows, watching Remington setting the bin on fire once he'd hauled the new Edwina into it. She'd made quite a *thunk* as her feet had hit the bottom — the bin must have been emptied recently — and it had taken Remington more than ten minutes to get a fire going. The silly prat hadn't thought to use the petrol from the can in the back of the car until he'd failed to light her up by using newspaper and matches.

"I heard you on the phone. Watched you when you rang her. I was *there*, outside the back of the chippy with you." Simon was so close to Remington that the individual pores on his nose stood out. They were blackened from the smoke.

"I didn't even take a phone with me, so that's wrong." Remington smirked. "You're making this up to see if I fall for your tricks. Well, I won't, because I didn't do anything like what you've said."

Simon had an evil card left to play. He hadn't wanted to use it — it meant scaring himself as well as Remington — but the little sod wasn't going to admit to anything, so needs must.

"This is your last chance to confess," Simon said.

"Confess to something I didn't do? No, Simon, I won't."

"All right then."

Simon walked away from Remington, into a far corner beside the vending machine. If he stood there, it might not be so bad.

"Edwina?" he called.

"No!" Remington darted forward, hands out in an imploring gesture. "Don't bring her back here. Please, don't do that."

"Edwina?" Simon said. "Remington's been a bad boy, and he needs punishing. Bring Trevor with you. The pair of you can sort him out because Lord knows I can't. He needs a beating then putting in the cupboard."

"Not Trevor." Remington sobbed, a stream of mucous dribbling out of his nose. He cuffed it away with his sleeve. "He sounds worse than Edwina — you told me all the horrible things they did to you. I don't want them to do that to me."

"Then admit you're lying," Simon yelled. "Just say you phoned the detective, then everything can go back to normal — except that I'll stay with you until all the Edwinas are gone. Just to make sure you kill them — I don't trust you anymore."

"Okay." Remington paced in front of the vending machine. "Okay, I rang her, but not to tell her about you. I did it to taunt her, like I always do."

"Like you *always* do?" Simon narrowed his eyes. How come this was the first time he was hearing about this? He shook his head. *Or has Remington told me before and I just forgot?*

"And when I devised that accident, it was to show Bethany that I couldn't get caught even though I was standing right by her." Remington shuddered, possibly from the shock of his admittance.

"The accident?"

Simon scrabbled to recall a bloody accident. He couldn't remember a thing. The idea of Edwina turning up here as a visitor must have addled his mind. Simon's thought processes blurred, and he couldn't work out what he knew for sure and what he didn't.

"You see what Edwina does to me?" Simon screeched. "Even the idea of her coming here has sent me doolally. And that's your fault, Remington — *yours!*" He grabbed handfuls of his hair and pulled. Rocked his torso backwards and forwards. "You need to get me my tablets. Go on, go upstairs and fetch them."

"I don't want to take them all for you. Don't make me have any, not tonight." Remington wrung his hands.

"I said *I* need them, shitface," Simon snarled. "All this Edwina visiting business has made me feel poorly."

Remington's shoulders slumped — in relief? — and he left the kitchen, his footsteps heavy on the stairs. He was probably walking slowly to waste time.

Simon stared over at Victoria, the mental healthcare bitch who'd told him he was close to being kept in the institution for even longer if he didn't stop hiding his tablets under his tongue then disposing of them when the nurses had left his room.

"What are *you* looking at?" He shivered, wedging himself farther into the corner.

She stood there in person, not against the wall as Remington's childish drawing. She looked at him in the way she always had before she'd been offed — with sympathy, her eyes damp where it seemed she was trying not to cry. Her blood had been much redder than the others — probably coloured by all those strawberry sweets she used to eat when Simon had an appointment with her. Suck, suck, suck, crunch, crunch, crunch.

Simon saw red. Red everywhere. He blinked a few times to clear his vision. "I asked you a question, lady. Answer me."

"It's time to stop doing these terrible things," she said. "It was time before you'd even started — you should never have done what you have. I should never have signed you off as fine to live here with Edwina. You belong in the hospital."

"I'm *in* the bloody hospital," he snapped. "Can't you see that? Remington made it for me. Look, there's a vending machine." He tapped the side of it with his knuckles. "And look at the waiting room in there. Magazines on the tables and everything. Can't you *see* them?"

Victoria nodded. "Yes, I see them, but this is all fake. It isn't the right kind of hospital for you."

"Piss off," he said.

The sound of Remington clambering down the stairs took Simon's attention away from the therapist. He stared at the doorway, and Remington appeared, a plastic box full of tablets clutched in one hand. He must have filled up all the compartments because there weren't that many in there the last time Simon checked.

Simon stretched his arm out. "Give them to me. And get me a drink. The sort Edwina liked."

Remington held the box out, and after Simon snatched it, Remington shuffled over to the cupboard on the wall to the left of the sink. He kept looking across at the corner as if he thought Simon was about to attack him or something. Simon had no time to think about that. He needed to do what had to be done.

A bout of shivers erupted through his body, and he emerged from the corner, cautious in case Victoria manhandled him and put him in one of those straitjacket things people like her stashed away in their cupboards.

*The cupboard . . .*

"Stay back." He held up his hand, palm outwards. "You just stay the hell away from me."

She frowned. "Remington, be careful."

Remington didn't look at her — he filled a pint glass with Edwina's tipple then walked towards Simon, holding the glass at chest height. He stood there like the dumb fucker he was and waited for Simon to take it.

"Put it on the worktop," Simon said.

Remington obeyed and edged his way over to the back door. He tried to squash himself into it — or through it, Simon wasn't sure — and Simon advanced, pouring the pills into his hand. There were too many and they overflowed, dropping to the floor and tapping as they jumped then came to rest.

"Don't come near me." Remington winced and screwed his eyes up tight.

"We have to take these." Simon curled his fingers over the tablets, creating a hole with his thumb and finger curled at the side of his hand. "So open your mouth and let me put them in."

Remington shook his head and opened his eyes. "No. I knew you were going to do this. I told the detective you'd do this. You said *you* needed to take them, otherwise I wouldn't have gone and got them."

"Ha! So you *did* tell her about me." Simon narrowed his eyes so he appeared scary — Remington didn't like it when he did that.

"Please don't stare at me with your eyes all slitty." Remington covered his face with his hands and peeked through the gaps between his fingers. "You're . . . you're just like Edwina when you do that."

Simon's heartbeat scattered. His chest burned from the pressure of the thuds, and he pinned Remington against the door with one hand at his throat. Remington gasped for breath, and as his mouth opened to its widest, Simon dropped the pills inside then clamped Remington's jaw closed.

"Eat them," he said. "Eat them all, shitface."

Remington let out choking noises. His eyes watered just like Victoria's — and she was shrieking like a bloody banshee behind him, trying to pull him off Remington. He shrugged her away and kicked back, sending her flying across the room. Simon pressed his body into Remington's, holding him in place, then let go of his throat to grab some of his hair and yank his head back.

"Swallow them," he commanded.

Remington shook his head, and saliva dribbled from the corners of his mouth. Simon slapped a hand over Remington's lips, watching his Adam's apple for signs of bobbing. Remington would have to give in eventually.

At last, with much fuss, snorting, and wriggling in an attempt to break free, Remington swallowed. His body convulsed — Simon guessed the tablets were stuck in his windpipe — and his eyes bulged, the red veins lightning flashes against the white. Simon massaged Remington's throat, and Remington swallowed yet again.

"That's it. All done now?" He pressed his nose to the end of Remington's. It was cold, just like when he pressed it to a windowpane.

Remington's face misted in front of him — that was like a windowpane thing, too — and Simon frowned. Maybe Victoria had crept up on them and had sprayed some of that vile air freshener. Yes, that was what the mist was. It seemed like Remington was outside now, on the other side of the glass.

"Now," Simon said. "There were quite a few of those tablets to manage, weren't there? Because you've been saving them up, not taking them every day, so it shouldn't be long before you fall asleep. I think you need a bit of sleep, don't you? Now you need to have a drink."

Remington shook his head and raised his hands. He tried to tug Simon's arms to release his hold, but Simon was ready for that and held him tighter. Remington slid down the door, Simon going down with him, and weirdly, Simon's head lightened. He felt sick and just about managed to reach up to the worktop and grab hold of the glass. He took his hand away from Remington's mouth then poured the drink into it. Remington spluttered and choked, but the majority of the liquid went down.

"That's it." Simon let Remington go and settled on the floor beside him. "I'm a bit tired myself, so we'll crawl to the cupboard, then I'll have a little sleep with you."

Simon's body seemed to sink into the floor as they plodded on hands and knees to the cupboard under the stairs, so different from the one Simon had been locked in as a child, but just as awful. Remington heaved, his body trying to expel the pills and drink, but Simon covered his mouth again.

They settled inside the cupboard, and Simon stared ahead at the canvas on the wall, made up of squares with dots in the middles. Skin from the Edwinas.

"Oh God . . ." Remington wailed.

*Sleep. Please, just sleep.*

* * *

*The Boy stared at the gift. It had been wrapped in yellowed newspaper and held together with rope instead of Sellotape. It was the first gift he'd ever had — or the first he could remember anyway. His friend at school had just handed it to him, and the Boy didn't know how the other lad had known it was his birthday. The Boy only knew because Edwina and Trevor had laughed when he'd got up this morning, saying he'd get no presents because he didn't deserve them.*

*This, then, his friend giving him a gift, disproved what they'd said, didn't it?*

*The Boy stared at the package. What could be inside it?*

*He looked up at Remington, the kid who had, for some reason, decided they should be friends since they'd started big school together, the only two people who knew each other from the nursery around the corner. Everyone else had gone to the other school. The posher one. Not the rowdy Middleton Road Primary that the Boy and Remington attended.*

*"Mrs Robins told everyone it was your birthday — she said about it yesterday when you went to the toilet. We're all going to sing to you later. On the carpet at story time." Remington covered his mouth with a chubby hand — he was portly whereas the Boy was slim. "I wasn't meant to tell you that. I'm sorry."*

*"It's all right."*

*The Boy held back tears. They were going to sing to him?*

*"I won't let anyone know you said." The Boy stroked the rope around the gift. "Did your mum buy the present for me?"*

*"No." Remington held his hands behind his back and swung his body from right to left. Like he felt silly. "I didn't have no money, so I wrapped that up because I wanted you to have a present."*

*Had someone told Remington that the Boy had never had a present before? Who would have done that? Confused, he scrunched his forehead up.*

*"Open it then," Remington said.*

*The Boy reached out to slip the rope off the package. Then he peeled back the newspaper— slowly, so slowly, because he wouldn't ever get another present again, he knew that. Inside was a lump of concrete, about the size of an apple.*

*"Do you like it?" Remington wrung his hands in front of him.*

*"I love it." And the Boy did. He loved it more than anything else in the world.*

*Rubble.*

* * *

Simon drifted, not the Boy anymore but the man he'd become. He realised now that the gift from the schoolboy, Remington, had been so special, so appreciated, that it had stuck in Simon's mind, affecting him in terrible ways. Had he attached the symbolism to Edwina as a way of expressing how he wished she'd been the one to buy him presents?

*I don't know. I don't know anything much anymore.*

He saw the concrete gifts that he'd tied to Edwina. He saw the criss-cross of rope. He saw the newspaper that he'd scrunched up and tried to light when he'd wanted to burn the latest Edwina. He thought of the extra padding he'd put on when he'd bought the phones and SIMs as Remington, so he'd appeared chubby, then how he'd gone in as his slimmer self to get one or two, but always with a scarf over his scarred face.

Remington had just been a passenger, a side of himself he wished he could be.

Then he saw nothing else. Nothing else at all except for blackness.

And it cuddled him like Edwina should have done.

# CHAPTER TWENTY-SIX

The air in the car park behind Whalebone's fish and chip shop was laden with the stench of smoke. Bethany stared at the wheelie bin. The partly melted lid had been propped up with what appeared to be a broomstick handle, and already SOCO in white overalls huddled around it, doing what had to be done. Grim tasks that no one should have to undertake. Isabelle hovered around, then spotted Bethany and came over.

"There's a rumour going about," Isabelle said.

"Is that right?" Bethany smiled. "I'd have let you know eventually. Been a bit busy, funny enough."

"We've got to get together in the Flapping Crow, say a proper goodbye." Isabelle's eyes watered above her face mask. "I'm going to have to get used to a new bloody DI now, aren't I?"

"And a DS," Mike said.

Isabelle shrieked, "What? Not you an' all?"

"Where Beth goes, I go," he said.

"Well, there's best mates for you." Isabelle gestured to the wheelie bin. "Back to work for me, but I'll grab you soon for a proper chat."

Bethany nodded.

"Bad shit, that," Mike said to her once Isabelle had gone.

"I assume you mean the burnt body, not us leaving." Bethany closed her eyes briefly. "And it'll get even worse if nothing comes up on that bloody Simon name. The Creep will keep doing this until he's either caught or gets bored."

"He could go on for a long time."

Bethany shook her head in despair. "With the woman from the canal, plus the others under the rubble, this bloke has had more evil than good going on in his life lately. He's seriously escalated. He has to be caught before the time frame between each kill gets shorter. Otherwise, not only will more needless lives be lost, but they'll be lost faster. Christ." She scrubbed a hand over her mouth. "Just look at that poor woman there."

It was Marsha Cobbs, Golden Glow's owner. Ursula had found a recent missing person's report. Marsha had opened the shop at the back but not the front, and a delivery had arrived, one that couldn't be signed for because she wasn't there. The driver had called it in as suspicious, seeing as he'd gained entry into the building. Then her mother had called in — she'd gone to the shop to see her daughter and, upon finding it closed but with the blinds up as if Marsha had been about to start her day, she'd visited Marsha's house. With no answer, she'd returned to the shop and checked round the back. Marsha's stubbed-out cigarette was there.

Bethany knew from the Butcher case that there was no CCTV behind the shops in that row, so they'd probably only spot the black BMW when it was driven past the end of the high street.

She stared ahead. The back of Marsha's neck rested on the lip of the bin, her head dangling over the side. Whoever had killed her had all but decapitated her. She could just make out her shoulders, the top of her chest, and an inch or two of the charred, awful skin just below. Her face was a mess of slices which had been stapled back together. Who the hell did that sort of thing?

She held back a retch.

"He's burned her because he can't dump her in the canal," Mike mused. "But why burn her? Why not just put her in the bin?"

"Because he's a clever bastard. Water and fire both remove evidence, although he didn't put her in properly, what with her face being exposed. Which makes me wonder, with what we discovered when we arrived . . . He said this Simon bloke is making him kill the women. Why start burning her then put the flames out? He *wants* to be caught, right? We saw the shop CCTV — we know there was only one man here."

"I agree, he obviously wants to be caught, otherwise it's pointless ringing us like he did."

"But whether he's been forced to kill them or not, he's still killed them, so it will be him who's put on trial. Although, of course, if there's proof that Simon has had a hand in this, then he'll be tried, too, but what I don't think this bloke realises is that no matter whether Simon instructed him to do this or not, he's still guilty. They both are."

"What if he's got some kind of disorder? So he's one person acting as two people at different times."

Bethany thought of what it must be like being two sides of one person at war with one another, the memory gaps they suffered when one side did something the other was unaware of. "Much as I hate to say it, because I'm not sticking up for the man, it must be awful to be him if that's the case. It could be argued that his behaviour isn't his fault — it's the fault of his condition if he has one."

"I know what you're saying. But whether he can't help himself or not, he's still done these things. Still taken lives. We can only hope he gets the help he needs once he's caught."

Glen appeared out of the shadows to their right, having walked down an alley leading from the street out the front of Whalebone's to the rear car park. "Bloody hell. I can see why you want to resign. It's a bit much at times, isn't it?"

"It is." Bethany smiled tightly. "Good for you in being able to keep going in this job. It's enough to send anyone to the funny farm." She explained the double personality angle.

"Oh. Right." Glen sighed. "Kind of makes sense."

Bethany's phone rang, and she answered it — Ursula.

"It's possibly a Simon Clements. He spent years in a mental facility after his stepfather went missing — he went a bit loopy because of it. He was released to live with his mother — his therapist signed him off as safe if he continued to take his meds."

"Give me his address."

Ursula did, and Bethany called it out so Mike could write it down.

"Thanks." She ended the call. "Right, us three are going to Simon Clements' address along with a few uniforms. Isabelle's here to oversee this lot." She nodded at SOCO working around Marsha and frowned, walking forward a bit to narrow her eyes and peer at the bin. "Christ, it was right there all along. What the Creep said about her being burnt at the place of his name. The bin's manufactured by Clements and Co. See it etched onto the front?"

She was pissed off she hadn't seen it before now.

"Simon's place," Bethany went on, "Suburbia, middle-of-the-road housing estate, house rented from the council by an Edwina Barry. I can't see this Simon bloke being out at this hour, unless he's looking for a new victim. Let's pray he isn't. Right—" she nudged Glen's arm — "you go and rustle up the uniforms we'll need, I'll go and get the car, bring it round."

With that sorted, Mike with her, Bethany drove to Simon's address, Glen following close behind. She parked a way down the road, close enough to see Simon's house but not enough to arouse suspicion. Most of the lights were off, but inside, a faint glow emitted through what she made out was an interior door that stood between two rooms.

"We'll stay put for now, until the uniforms show up," Bethany said. "Hopefully, they'll have the sense not to come into the street with the blues flashing and sirens blaring."

"What about Glen?" Mike asked.

"Just going to ring him now. He's parked up behind us, look." Bethany got her phone out and made the call.

"Uniforms know not to arrive all guns blazing, don't they?" She nodded. "I should have known you'd tell them how to proceed, sorry. Right, yes, good idea," Bethany went on. "We'll take the front — me, Mike, and a uniform. You and the other three uniforms take the back. We don't want to let this Simon bloke know we're here until we're all in position, so I'll wait before I knock or ring the bell if he has one."

A police patrol car sailed past.

"Oh, for fuck's *sake*! Look at those sodding prats." Bethany shoved her phone in her pocket. She got on the radio. "All police in the vicinity of Denim Road, Simon Clements' address, get your cars out of bloody view!" As she climbed from the car, she stared in the direction of the police vehicle, gritting her teeth. She shut the door quietly and opened the boot, took two stab vests out, and strode to Glen's car.

Mike got out and followed. He took a stab vest from her and put it on. She was nervous that the vest would be the only thing stopping Simon Clements from jabbing a knife into their bellies, backs, or hearts.

Glen joined them on the pavement, leaning inside his car to drag a vest from the back seat then slipping it on over his shirt.

"I did tell them not to do that — come near the house," Glen said.

"Too late to do anything about it now." Bethany stared down the street again.

The driver of the police car had made a three-point turn and was coming back their way. *What?* As it passed, Bethany jerked her thumb to indicate that they park out of sight. Her blood pressure was rising. She'd explode before long if they kept up this amateur behaviour.

"Deep breath," Mike said. "It isn't worth getting yourself in a state over."

Bethany nodded, one quick bow of the head, then walked to the street entrance, leaving Glen behind to keep an eye on the house. Mike walked beside her. The guilty uniforms had exited their car, and the second duo had already done as Glen had told them, staying out of sight of Clements' house. All four coppers stood on the pavement, and she could tell which two had disobeyed orders. Their faces were red, and they stared down at their feet.

"If it wasn't so early in the morning and we didn't need to be quiet, I'd blow up on you," Bethany whispered to them. "Of all the stupid things . . ." She stepped closer to the offenders. "Look at me. Heads up. This isn't your usual bust, understand? This is a *killer*, got it?" She stared at all four in turn. "Do you have your stab vests on? No, I see you don't. What part of your training did you actually take in? Any of it?"

No one answered.

Bethany tutted. "You three will go round the back with Glen." She pointed to the fourth man. "You, me, and Mike, we'll be knocking on the front door. Now, you *know* how this kind of thing works."

The four men nodded.

"Right, vests on, then join us round the corner." Bethany jogged into Denim Road. Back with Glen, Mike next to her, she said, "Just to be on the safe side, there might well be this Simon plus the one who's actually doing the killing. The Creep. While Simon has issues, it doesn't mean the Creep wasn't telling the truth in that there's himself and another man. We'll proceed with caution."

Glen beckoned the other policemen over and led them across the road.

Following, Bethany and Mike reached the front door. As directed, one officer stayed with them while the other three went down the side of the house with Glen. The sound of a gate opening churned her stomach. She lifted her hand ready to rap the door with her knuckles.

"Pills spilt on the floor in the kitchen!" Glen shouted.

Bethany elbowed the glass panel in the front door, at the corner. It took several attempts for the pane to crack, then the copper belatedly handed her his baton. Bethany used it to smack out the glass and reached inside to unlock the door. She turned down the handle to gain access, but the door wouldn't budge.

"Bloody bolts, I'll bet," she said.

She stood back then kicked the door, repeating the move several times before it gave way and flung open. Bethany surged inside, the copper next, then Mike. The place stank, and she breathed through her mouth, adrenaline jumping into her system. Protruding from a cupboard under the stairs, she spotted a hand. She went closer and peered inside. A man, legs covered in tracksuit bottoms. Bethany went down on her knees and checked for a pulse.

"Faint but there," Bethany said.

The policeman who'd entered with her rang in for an ambulance, and Mike stepped back and out of the way as Bethany pulled the man out and put him in the recovery position. She checked out the cupboard. At the end, mounted on the wall, was a canvas, but only part of it had anything on it. Small squares with dots in the middle, placed next to one another like mosaic tiles. They were staggered in the bottom-right corner, upside-down steps, not enough tiles to finish the piece.

She backed out, making a mental note to get it taken in. She moved into the kitchen, to a far corner beside a vending machine — *what the fuck?* — and took stock of the rest of the room. She vaguely registered Glen and the other officers entering, and footsteps banged on the stairs. But her attention was on a stretch of wall opposite. The figure of a woman had been drawn there, her face some kind of magazine printout, and words had been scrawled in red paint — at least she thought it was paint.

*Edwina Barry is a nasty fucking whore. Kill. Kill. Kill.*

She felt sick. Yes, enough was definitely enough.

She couldn't take any more of this shit.

# CHAPTER TWENTY-SEVEN

Everyone had gathered in the Flapping Crow, and Bethany found it difficult to swallow the lump in her throat. It was quite the turnout.

"There's more people here than I thought would come," she whispered to Mike.

"Why wouldn't they? You're lovely."

"So are you — it's your leaving do as well, remember."

Isabelle came over, three sheets to the wind already, her boyfriend, Aradul, hanging off her arm. "I don't want to work with anyone else." She stuck out her bottom lip. "I love you, woman. Please don't leave me."

Bethany's eyes leaked. "It's not like I'm leaving completely. I'll still keep in contact, and we can meet up in here for a drink."

"When you want my opinion on your fancy new PI cases, yeah."

"Don't be bitter, there's a dear." Bethany smiled.

Isabelle swiped at her cheeks. "It's just . . . we have such a good rapport. What if the new DI dogs me off, pokes their nose in?"

"They have to poke their nose in," Bethany said.

"You know what I mean." Isabelle sniffed and glanced to her right. "Well, now, Elvis has entered the building."

"Stop it!" Bethany turned to smile at Presley.

If he'd heard Isabelle calling him Elvis, he'd chosen not to comment. Those two always bickered, and Bethany had to admit she'd miss that. They all worked so well together, and hopefully the new DI and DS would fit in seamlessly. She'd hate to think of Isabelle and Presley having their nerves grated by a newbie.

"Thanks for coming, Pres," Bethany said. "I know you don't like doing the pub thing with work colleagues."

"I did it before, on the Hide and Seek case, and besides, this is a bit different." Presley gave a rare smile. "I suppose I'll hear from you anyway, for advice, but I'd rather hoped I'd taught you enough about manners of death for you to manage without me."

"You taught me loads, and I'm grateful."

"What are you drinking?" he asked.

"I'm moving on to lemonade." She winced. "Make it a tonic water. Simon had a thing about lemonade."

She thought back to his interview once he'd had his stomach pumped. A mental health nurse had been in attendance, what with his previous stint in a facility, and in the bed of a real hospital, not the bizarre one in his home, he'd gabbled about being Simon, Remington, and the Boy who'd liked lemonade at Mrs Saunders' house.

That name had led them to finding out quite a bit regarding Simon. Mrs Saunders still lived in the street where he'd grown up, and she knew all about Edwina and her husband, Trevor, although Trevor had gone missing prior to a drug bust, which had proved fruitless, and he hadn't been seen since.

Simon had solved that puzzle, saying the Boy had starved him and dumped him in the canal with the help of a man called Runner. Bethany had heard of him, one of the men who worked for Uncle Crack, the local drug lord, and she'd had him hauled in for questioning. Of course, the Transit Simon had mentioned that was used to transport the body was long gone, rusty pieces on the scrap heap, and as it was ages ago, they had no proof Runner had even had anything to do with it. The house had been renovated, the cupboard knocked out in the dining room, the floor cemented over, so unless Kribbs decided to have the layer beneath checked out for Trevor's DNA, that side of things would be put to bed.

Kribbs had refused to have the canal dredged again to find Trevor's bones.

While she'd been stuck in her head, Presley had bought her tonic water and handed it over. Thanks given, she looked around at the others gathered, who stood by the bar or sat at nearby tables.

Fran and Leona chatted animatedly with Glen — they'd all just finished reading a diary that had been found in Simon's house, so the talk was probably about that. Some disturbing things had come to light. A Mr Collier was mentioned, him coming to see the Crying Lad, which was a heartbreaking name, and Bethany knew his daughter as well as the woman would allow her to. She also knew of John, the policeman, and the news that this case was related to Collier had thrown Bethany for a loop.

She shrugged it all off. She shouldn't be concerning herself with it now. The paperwork had been filed, Simon had been admitted into a facility, and that was the end of it. If anything else came to light, Fran and Leona could sort it out with the new DI.

Bethany checked the others were having a good time. There stood Tory Yates, Nicola Eccles, Penny Dickens, and Jack Moller. The latter Bethany hadn't really got to know but had worked with him on occasion. All lovely PCs, along with Glen, and people she'd miss, but to be honest, if she got PI work in, she'd probably have to speak to them about things if she needed their help.

Alice Jacobs, the FLO, nattered with Kribbs and Rob. Ursula wasn't there — she was manning the front desk, as usual at this time of night, and Bethany had already said a tearful goodbye to her earlier.

Angela Hill, the *Herald's* editor, sat with Peter Uxbridge, the Regional Crime writer, and Bethany would bet he'd put together a scathing report after this, bidding her good riddance. He'd always picked at her in his articles, and she wouldn't be sorry to leave him to his own devices. The only bugbear she had was that she'd never found out who the leak was in the station, giving him information.

She took in all her workmates one by one, asking herself if any of them would have passed details to him. She couldn't see it, to be honest, so it might well be a SOCO, considering the info given out had to be someone in the know, closer to the investigation than a PC. She'd put that to Isabelle if she didn't think the woman would be offended — Isabelle ran a tight ship and would hate it if one of her three teams were involved.

*It's not your business now anyway. Forget it after tonight. Walk away.*

"All right there?" someone said behind her.

Bethany turned to face a woman she hadn't seen for a while. Rita, the barmaid from the Lamb Shank, stood there in all her garish glory, the usual make-up plastered on, her gregarious clothes stuck to her curvy body.

"Hello, you!" Bethany gave her a hug. "How are you?"

The last time Bethany had heard of Rita, she'd walloped some fella over the head with a bottle of Becks for pinching her nipple. She'd caused affray in the pub, and the bloke had been nicked for sexual assault.

"Not too bad," Rita said. "I heard on the grapevine you're leaving so thought I'd nip here and see you." She glanced about. "See what the competition's like as well." She sniffed. "The Flapping Crow is not the Lamb Shank. Can't believe you're having your do here."

Bethany laughed. "Mike organised it, blame him."

"Oh, I bloody well will!" She strutted off towards Mike, who propped up the bar with Presley. "Mike! Mike! I want a word with you . . ."

Bethany smiled through tears of joy and sadness. She'd been so lucky to be involved with all these people. There had been ups and down, yes, times she'd wanted to brain every one of them at some point, but they'd become her friends as well as colleagues, people who made up her day-to-day life, filling the giant hole Vinny had left when he'd died.

"Would you look who's leaving us," someone shouted. "Walking away. Got to be Shadwell. I walked away from here an' all . . ."

Bethany spun to face the door. "Tracy!"

Tracy Collier walked towards her, arms out. "Don't you go getting ideas that I've gone soft in giving you a cuddle," she said, gathering her into her arms. "People will start thinking I've had a personality transplant."

Bethany hugged her back. "What are *you* doing here?" This was the last person she'd expected to see.

"Mike got hold of us." She nodded at Damon, her DS and boyfriend, who was just coming in. "And of course, I knew you were leaving because it has something to do with me. I've got to interview for a new DI and DS — that's what happens when you run Serious Crimes. Whoever it is has big shoes to fill." She paused and looked into Bethany's eyes. Leant forward to whisper, "I wish I had your balls. To leave. Walk away." She pulled back and let Bethany go.

"Why don't you then?"

Tracy shrugged. "Reasons. And you added another one to the pile, what with the info about the Crying Lad. I didn't expect that, I can tell you. That man who called himself my father, and that wanker, John, didn't seem to be into boys. Just shows you what you don't know, eh? So as well as working my usual cases, I'm working the Collier case on the side. I can't leave until I've found all those kids and made sure they're all right."

"I understand." Bethany sensed it was time to change the subject. "What are you drinking?"

"I'm not. Designated driver. I can't stand Shadwell, for obvious reasons, and being here drunk isn't my cuppa. I like to be on guard."

Bethany supposed, if you'd been brought up here and all your worst nightmares remained in town, you wouldn't want to feel out of control when you went back. "I'm sorry about all that happened to you."

Tracy nodded. "Get lost. We're not going down that road. So, I hope you're going to bend my ear if you need me in the future. It'll be weird without you on the end of a phone line, reporting in, me letting you get on with it. Shit." She raised her eyes to the ceiling. "I'm going to have to let the new DI know I'm not into running the show in Shadwell. Reckon I'll get away with just asking them to phone me with updates like you did?"

Bethany shrugged. "Maybe you'll get an applicant who prefers it that way."

"Hmm, I'd bloody better." She glanced over at Damon, who spoke to Mike and Presley. "I knew he'd leave with you. Best mates, aren't you."

Bethany nodded. "He's like my brother. Couldn't have done half of what I did without him." Her eyes misted. "Love him to bits."

Kribbs turned, holding a pint glass up. He tapped a cocktail stirrer against it, shouting, "Can I have a bit of attention, please?"

"Oh shit," Tracy said. "The goodbye speech."

"Exactly what I didn't want," Bethany muttered out of the side of her mouth.

"Tough." Tracy winked. "You leave us, this is your penance."

Kribbs looked over at Bethany. "Now then, as you know, we're all gathered here for our wonderful DI, and let me tell you, there isn't another one like her, nor will there ever be."

"Charming!" Tracy said.

Everyone laughed.

Kribbs gave her a nod. "We're all aware of how much Bethany has put into her role as Detective Inspector, working her backside off, all in the name of justice. She's like a dog with a bone and won't let go until she finds the criminal she's after, and she's sacrificed a lot of her life in doing so. Now it's time to relax a bit, to step away from her sometimes gruesome role and smell the roses. She's not interested in being a desk jockey like me, so she's off to pastures new. I don't want to get all mushy, but I'm going to miss you, Bethany, and of course, our Mike, who's done more than necessary at all times alongside you. This is a double whammy, losing you both, but we wish you the best and hope to keep in touch." He raised his glass higher. "To Mike Wilkins!"

Everyone raised theirs and repeated, "To Mike Wilkins!"

"And to dear Bethany Smith, one of the nicest, most dedicated people we'll ever know."

"To Bethany Smith!"

She couldn't see, couldn't hear for the emotion swamping her. For a fleeting second, she asked herself: *What have I done?* The mist over her eyes cleared, and everyone surged forward, enveloping her in a massive group hug, lots of cheers and people jumping up and down. Tracy reached across and gripped her hand, and they stared at one another, Tracy nodding as if to say: *Go, be free while you can.* Bethany nodded back, tears falling, and she sobbed. For how she'd miss her workmates, the job, the camaraderie, but most of all, for closing Vinny's chapter and moving on.

While he'd always be with her, she had to let him go.

She had to live the life he'd want her to. Happy, unafraid, and content.

# EPILOGUE

Their new office was kitted out and ready for them to use. They'd chosen one above a row of shops. The rent was low for the main room with a kitchenette to the left and a toilet to the right. Two desks sat at the rear, each in front of a window, and beside the entry door was a leather sofa and one matching chair for prospective clients. A large fluffy beige rug in front of the furniture gave that area a comfortable air, as did a trendy coffee table with a few magazines displayed on top.

The sight of it gave Bethany a bit of a chill. Simon Clements' living room had just such a thing, the space kitted out to resemble a hospital waiting room.

*Crazy as anything, that one.*

"Looking good in here," Mike said.

Bethany smiled at him. "Bet you didn't really think you'd ever see this day, did you?"

She hadn't thought she'd see it so soon either, that she'd actually go through with it. She'd handed in her notice, and instead of resting and regrouping for a month, so she didn't get caught up by grief at last, she'd gone straight out and looked for premises and applied for her licence, worried that if she didn't, the bug that had bitten her to become a private investigator might bog off and not come back.

"I knew you'd had enough. For good." Mike smiled. "I'm just relieved Kribbs didn't give me too much grief about leaving, too."

"Here's hoping our new jobs will suit us better."

"Yeah, and that my new boss won't be a demanding arsehole."

Bethany feigned hurt by frowning and clutching a hand to her heart. "Oh, I won't be a demanding arsehole."

Mike laughed. "You will. You'll want this business to succeed, otherwise, you'll blame yourself for leaving the police, and you won't want to admit you might be wrong by doing that."

"Hey, are you saying this is bad thing?" Bethany gestured to their office.

"Nope, far from it. Been nice not to have to deal with murder." Mike moved to the sofa then sat on it, a big old sigh coming out of him. "I knew we'd been pressed for time before, that everything revolved around work, but now we've had a few days to get this done, I realised how damn tired I was."

Bethany joined him, sitting close. "Yep. Always squeezing real life in, never living it."

She was so bloody happy. The weight of the world had jumped off her shoulders pretty quickly after she'd walked out of the police station for the last time. She'd thought the job would plague her still, that she'd hanker after it, hanker after working with Fran, Leona, Glen, Nicola, Isabelle, Presley, God, so many people who were dear to her, but no, as soon as she'd arrived home after the leaving party, she'd sighed with extreme relief and hadn't been able to believe that she was actually free. It had taken about a week for her to stop expecting the phone to ring, or for her sleep to be disturbed by the information on a case swirling inside her head. But since then? It was kind of like she'd never been a policewoman — it had been a different life, and she had to start a new one.

*But it might be like Mike said the other day. I'm shutting it out. Self-preservation. Like I shut Vinny's death out and pretended he was still here, somewhere, only I just couldn't see him, be with him.*

Whatever it was, Bethany was enjoying the different pace, the idea that she could pick and choose whatever jobs she took on. No more gruelling murder cases. No more Kribbs and his budget or ex-wife rants. No more chasing killer's arses, trying to stop them before they murdered someone else. No more victims to look at, sick to her stomach at the sight of them. No more families, all of them bereft and wrecked, their lives never to be the same again.

*Heaven.*

"Do you think our remaining business savings will be enough to see us through the first case?" Mike asked. "Because I read on the internet that expenses can be pretty high for PIs. Petrol, hotel rooms, food, paying people for information."

"Yep, we've got a couple of grand left after doing this place up, haven't we, so I don't think we need to worry just yet. And besides, I was meant to tell you, I plan on asking for a retainer up front — that's usual, but I want ours to be a bigger one. Once the retainer amount has been used up on expenses, the client will pay the next instalment. It'll work itself out." Bethany took a notebook out of her pocket. "That reminds me, we haven't sat still long enough to work out a basic price list."

"Hmm, we ran before we could walk. All those adverts in the papers and whatnot, and you don't even have a ball-park figure to offer anyone if that phone bloody rings."

"If it rings, I reckon I'll shit myself." Bethany rubbed a kink in the back of her neck. "But at the same time I'll want to punch the air. A month off was enough for me. I'm looking forward to getting back to work. Even if it's just searching for a runaway dog or something minor like that." She shuddered at the memory of Simon Clements splayed out on his cupboard floor. She tried to block the visual but couldn't. "If we ever get involved in a case where there's a killer, make me refuse it, all right?"

"Yep." Mike nodded. "Dealing with that kind of thing isn't what we agreed."

"I wonder if the regulated medication has helped Clements." Bethany had discovered from Mrs Saunders what kind of life Clements had lived. It was no wonder he was crazy. It didn't excuse what he'd done, but it explained a lot.

"Probably." Mike shrugged. "And if it hasn't? Not our problem anymore. He's off the streets, and that's what matters."

A phone on one of the desks jangled, and they both jumped. Mike shot up, moving as though he was going to answer it, then decided against it.

"You do it," he said.

"I can't." Bethany grimaced.

"Why. Shit yourself, have you?"

Bethany laughed. "Not literally no, but—"

"Will you get a move on before it stops ringing? Christ, this could be our first case."

Bethany got up and raced to the desk. Heart pounding, she lifted the receiver, excited yet daunted at the same time. "Smith and Wilkins Private Investigations, how may I help you?"

"Good morning. My name's Elizabeth Grafton. I wonder if you have time to look into something for me?"

"Of course, Ms Grafton." Bethany gave Mike the thumbs-up. "If you could give me a rough idea of the problem, then I can decide whether we can help you."

"It's my husband. He's been missing for a while now, and the police aren't doing anything to find him."

"I see." Bethany's hackles went up at what the woman had implied. She knew what went on behind the scenes, and although it might appear that the police weren't doing anything, they actually were. Still, that wasn't anything to do with her now. "Would you prefer to come into the office to discuss it, Mrs Grafton? We have all morning free."

"That would be wonderful," she said. "I know where you are and I'll be along shortly, I'm only round the corner. Say two minutes?"

"Two minutes suits us fine. See you then." Bethany placed the phone back in its dock. She looked at Mike. "Fuck, what have we done?"

"We *can* make a go of this, you know," he said. "Have faith."

Bethany walked over to him and stole a hug. "I don't know what I'd do without you urging me on."

"It's the same for me. Without you . . . well . . ."

Bethany squeezed him and drew back. "We're in this together and always will be, right?"

"Right. Always. This is our dream. We can do this."

A sharp knock sounded on the door.

"There's only one way to find out," Bethany said.

"Too right. So let's get this show on the road."

**THE END**

## THE JOFFE BOOKS STORY

We began in 2014 when Jasper agreed to publish his mum's much-rejected romance novel and it became a bestseller.

Since then we've grown into the largest independent publisher in the UK. We're extremely proud to publish some of the very best writers in the world, including Joy Ellis, Faith Martin, Caro Ramsay, Helen Forrester, Simon Brett and Robert Goddard. Everyone at Joffe Books loves reading and we never forget that it all begins with the magic of an author telling a story.

We are proud to publish talented first-time authors, as well as established writers whose books we love introducing to a new generation of readers.

We won Trade Publisher of the Year at the Independent Publishing Awards in 2023. We have been shortlisted for Independent Publisher of the Year at the British Book Awards for the last four years, and were shortlisted for the Diversity and Inclusivity Award at the 2022 Independent Publishing Awards. In 2023 we were shortlisted for Publisher of the Year at the RNA Industry Awards.

We built this company with your help, and we love to hear from you, so please email us about absolutely anything bookish at: feedback@joffebooks.com.

If you want to receive free books every Friday and hear about all our new releases, join our mailing list: www.joffebooks.com/contact

And when you tell your friends about us, just remember: it's pronounced Joffe as in coffee or toffee!

## ALSO BY EMMY ELLIS

**DI BETHANY SMITH**

Book 1: THE COLD CALL KILLER
Book 2: THE CREEPY-CRAWLY KILLER
Book 3: THE SCREWDRIVER KILLER
Book 4: THE SCORCHED SKIN KILLER
Book 5: THE STREET PARTY KILLER
Book 6: THE CANDY CANE KILLER
Book 6.5: THE SECRET SANTA KILLER
Book 7: THE MEAT HOOK KILLER
Book 8: THE BLADE KILLER
Book 9: THE SLEDGEHAMMER KILLER

**DETECTIVE CAROL WREN MYSTERIES**

Book 1: SPITE YOUR FACE
Book 2: HOLD YOUR BREATH
Book 3: GUILT BURNS HOLES
Book 4: BEST SERVED COLD
Book 5: BLOOD RUNS DEEP

Printed in Great Britain
by Amazon

46673839R00108